DADDY
BIG BUCKS

To Bernice & Seymour
Thanks for being our
friends for the past
30+ years
Bob 11/20/87

DADDY
BIG BUCKS

Robert Waite

BENIN PUBLISHING COMPANY
Teaneck, New Jersey

Library of Congress Catalog Card No. 87-90664

ISBN: 0-9609948-2

BENIN PUBLISHING COMPANY
802 Columbus Drive
Teaneck, New Jersey 07666 U.S.A.

Author's Note

Since slavery, there has always been a Big Bucks in every Black neighborhood—desperately conniving, in some cases, to put two pennies together; owning, in others, a number of profitable businesses. He (or she) is a character cut from the same cloth as Rockefeller, Carnegie, Ford, and other giants of American Industry.

The great tragedy is not that Big Bucks and other Blacks like him are unknown in *mainstream* America, but that, to *Black* Americans, dazzled by lawyers, and other professionals, these entrepreneurs remain invisible.

CHAPTER ONE

"Shine?"

The tall thin man, hunched over his large mahogany desk, lurched, startled, in response. His arm struck a steaming cup of coffee and sent it sprawling over his neatly typed report.

Standing there in the doorway stood an elf-like man, his face resembling a prune that had been in the sun too long. The light made his straightened hair glisten. In one hand he held his shoe shine box; the other was propped against the door frame.

"Damn," the thin man exclaimed, trying to extract the report from the spilled coffee. The smell of the beverage rose, heavy in the air.

"Guess I woke you up," the shoe shine man replied in an amused laugh. He disappeared as quickly as he had come.

Suddenly the thin man leapt from his chair, shooting a hand into his pocket to shield his member from the hot coffee that had soaked through his crotch, the searing pain

1

making its way from groin to stomach. He performed a slow jig until it subsided. Finally, he looked in horror at the dark spreading circle. Damn, he thought, people'll swear I've gone in my pants.

"Problems?"

He looked up to see his secretary, Bridget, framed in the doorway with a wide quizzical smile on her finely chiseled face, which, with her violet eyes, bore an amazing resemblance to the young Elizabeth Taylor. She was well-proportioned and had an enormous bosom that she often enhanced with low cut blouses. There was a mischievous quality in her eyes.

"Look what he did to this report you just typed," Bert snarled.

"Who?" Her smile faded as she focused on it.

"That shoe shine man, sneaking up and scarin' the hell out of me. I asked you to keep everybody out till I finished this report."

A look of defiance crept over her face. "You sent me down to the Chairman's office, remember?"

"Yeah, yeah," he admitted hurriedly. "See what you can do to fix this, will you? I'm going to grab a bite."

Amusement returned to her voice. "Like that?"

"I gotta eat. Maybe my jacket will hide it." He pulled on his suit coat and shoved his hand into a pocket, shifting the front of the jacket until it covered the stain.

"That'll really attract attention," declared Bridget. She walked over to the small closet by the door and said, "Try this," bringing his rain coat and holding it out to him.

"I can't wear this in the cafeteria," he complained, following her out to her cubicle as she returned to her typewriter. He watched her gingerly fingering the stained report. She let out a deep sigh, her bosom almost touching the keyboard. Realizing he would get no more sympathy from her, he left for the cafeteria.

Bert Davis was the thin man's name. He had recently been named the Director of Planning for American Instruments, a worldwide manufacturer of control devices. Bert was almost six and a half feet tall and wore what was left of his hair in a frizzy afro. He grunted to the other executives he passed in the stark hallway of tan walls and nondescript flooring, ignoring the quizzical smiles on their faces, seeing his raincoat being worn on a hot, sunny day.

The smell of overcooked food and dank kitchen met him as he got off the elevator two floors beneath his and joined the cafeteria line. He glumly eyed the unappetizing food that lay in the steam pans surrendering a medley of scents that confirmed his suspicions. A stout woman behind the counter, her eyes magnified by thick glasses, looked at him. In a sing-song West Indian accent, pointing her large spoon at a strange-looking reddish stew, she said, ''Need some of dat for de belly—stay wit you.'' Bert shook his head.

''No pleasin' you today, I see,'' she muttered, rolled her magnified fish-like eyes toward the ceiling, then turned to the next person in line. He opted for the salad bar. As he entered the dining area, his eyes fastened on one table in the sea of fifty identical others, white, plastic-topped, each with four dull red chairs, salt and pepper shakers, and a black napkin dispenser. The windows that were never cleaned lent the room a dismal look even on such a bright day.

Three men were sitting at the table Bert was making his way to; Jim, the smallest of the three, was Bert's best friend, and headed the Personnel Department. His round, brown, cherubic face that crinkled when he smiled reminded

3

Bert of Gandhi's. Harry, Jim's second in command, wore a yellow-green bold striped tie that clashed with his blue plaid suit. His plump, beefy-red face was wreathed with long white sideburns. He sang out, "Hey, hey, look—here comes the company guru."

The third man was plump, had deep dimples, and a dreamy faraway look. He paused, his fork full of pie half way to his mouth, and gave Bert a forced smile. Bert thought his name was Mike.

"Got room for me?" Bert asked, sliding his tray onto the cold Formica, not waiting for an answer. There was a scraping of chairs as they moved around.

"Figure it's gonna rain?" asked Jim, putting down the bulletin he was reading and tightening his red silk tie. It set off his impeccable pearl grey suit perfectly.

Harry scratched his protruding belly and said, "Of course, don't you see his rain coat?"

"It was an accident," muttered Bert as he slipped off the coat and hurriedly slid into his seat.

"Looks to me like you couldn't make the toilet," Jim observed, and the table, except for Bert, broke out in laughter.

"Very funny," Bert mumbled; then, in a more dramatic voice, added, "Laugh if you want. If my economic report is anywhere near right, you won't have anything to laugh about."

"What's it look like?" Harry asked, suddenly sober.

"Not good," Bert snapped, glad to have gained an audience to test out the presentation he would deliver to the Board at the end of the month. "The dollar is still strong as hell, and Japan is killing us in Europe and here at home. We've just gotta get our cost down, across the board."

"God, he sounds just like Daddy Big Bucks, doesn't he?" asked Harry, leaning back in his chair and looking at his companions.

Jim folded the bulletin and stuck it in his pocket. In a serious voice, he said, "Sounds like he's stolen Big Bucks' material." A chorus of laughter followed.

"I think he has," Harry confirmed, bringing the front legs of his seat down, his red face taking on an intense look.

Bert, annoyed to find he was still the butt of their jokes, decided to remain silent and wait them out. Jim finished his ice cream, a smile breaking through. Harry's face was obscured by the coffee cup he was draining. And the third man, the one Bert thought was called Mike, announced he was going up to get an ice cream bar. Bert silently ate his salad.

As the third man was returning, Bert asked, "Who is this Big Bucks?"

"Thought you'd never ask," Harry replied. The three men focused on Bert. "The shoe shine man."

"*Shoe* shine man? Not the little Black guy with the conked hair?"

"Conked?" Harry asked.

"He straightens his hair," Jim responded. Then he said to Bert, "Same guy."

"And *he* knows about the economy?"

"Said exactly what *you* said," Mike replied.

"Hell," said Harry, trying to keep a straight face, "just this morning, while he shined my shoes, he gave me his latest economic forecast. His sounded so much like yours that we thought you might have stolen his material."

Jim struggled unsuccessfully to choke down his laughter. "You might say," as he gasped for breath, "he's a down home economist," at which all three broke into peals of laughter.

The whole cafeteria was watching their table. Bert looked around and asked, "Do we have to be this loud?" The question was ignored. Harry doubled up with laughter,

Mike was gasping for breath. Jim recovered first. "His real name is Hiawatha Jackson. But Daddy Big Bucks is his name, and money is his game."

"You know, Bert," Harry said, wiping his eyes, "you may want him on your staff, since you both think alike." Another round of laughter began.

"I'm not in the habit of consulting shoe shine men for my economic forecasts," Bert answered in a huff, pushing away his half-eaten salad.

"Gee, that's too bad," Jim mumbled. "You might learn something."

"I heard that," Bert said, his voice half serious. "I don't have to sit here and be insulted." He carefully measured two spoons of sugar into his coffee.

Mike, still laughing, excused himself.

"Why, that bugger came into my office and made me spill my coffee. That's why the raincoat," Bert ended lamely, realizing no one was going to accept it.

"You're saying Big Bucks made you go in your pants?" Harry asked innocently. A cafeteria worker cleared the dishes from the table and wiped it clean with a wet smelly rag.

"Drop dead," Bert growled when the worker had finished.

"Now don't get mad," Jim said placatingly. "Like most people, you seriously underestimate Big Bucks. He is *not* your ordinary shoe shine man."

"Right," said Harry. "We've studied Big Bucks for some time now. He's not just an old, ignorant shoe shine man. He's an entrepreneur in the classic sense of American capitalism. It's a matter of perspective."

"Bull!" Bert snapped, his cup poised in mid-air. "He can't even shine shoes. I've seen what he calls a shine."

"There you have it!" exclaimed Harry, triumphantly leaning forward in his seat. "How many shoe shine men do you know that can make a can of shoe polish last a whole year? I tell you, that's the stuff great businessmen are made of."

"Big deal, so he's too cheap to buy polish. This makes him an entrepreneur?"

"That's only the tip of the iceberg," Jim explained. "Suppose I were to tell you that Big Bucks owns the shoe shine franchise for thirty office buildings here in Manhattan, and that each Monday morning he makes the rounds and collects twenty dollars from each man."

"You're kidding!"

"Would we lie to you?" Harry asked, crumpling up his napkin and depositing it on the clean Formica.

"Seriously," said Jim, "that's why he's called Big Bucks. Seems that Hiawatha Jackson likes to have big bucks early on Monday morning. Claims it gets the week off to the right start."

"I'll be damned," Bert said grudgingly.

"Hold on. That's not all," Harry said, seeing that Bert's curiousity was piqued. "He also sells Watkins products."

"Watkins? The company that used to sell door to door in Black neighborhoods? I didn't know they were still in business."

Harry deferred to Jim, who said, "Oh yeah, he's always trying to get me to buy laundry soap from him. But the real hooker is that he's in real estate—claims he owns an apartment building over in Queens."

"And don't forget he's over sixty-five and collects his social security," Harry added, buttoning his coat over his bulging middle.

The short Brown man nodded his head. "So," he continued, "with a financial empire like that, his name comes pretty naturally."

The cafeteria was almost empty; the workers eyed them impatiently as they slouched in their chairs, engrossed in conversation.

7

"Yeah," Harry mused, "Big Bucks is quite a character. Got a boat, a Mercedes, and a motorcycle..."

"A motorcycle?"

"Yeah," said Harry with a smile, "he tools around upstate on weekends, with his girl on the back."

"Isn't he a little old for that?"

"Not if you run around with young chicks."

"I warned you," Jim said, flicking the lint off his grey suit, "Big Bucks is not your run-of-the-mill shoe shine man. 'Course, I don't want to give the impression that our hero is without blemishes."

"Such as?" Bert asked, riveted to his seat.

"For beginners," Harry said, "he's no equal opportunity employer. We had to give him a long lecture on that today."

"Oh, come on," Bert said sarcastically. "How many White people today are looking to shine shoes?"

Jim and Harry looked at each other. "You don't understand," said Jim. "Big Bucks doesn't hire Blacks."

Bert snorted.

"Honest to God," Harry agreed, raising his right hand. "Said they don't really want to work."

"Seriously?" Bert asked, turning to Jim.

"Spent the whole morning trying to get him to see the error of his ways. I suspect we weren't too successful."

"I wonder if he has any Black tenants?" Harry pondered. "Well, he's consistent," the red-faced man continued, "I'll say that for him. His ideas on women are just as bad."

"He's a real chauvinist," declared Jim. "He claims he never keeps a girlfriend after she turns twenty-five."

"Oh, come off it."

"God's own truth," Harry confirmed. "Claims you can't trust them over twenty-five."

"I don't believe that. What in the hell would any woman want with an old shrunken prune like that?"

8

"You'd be surprised. Some of them right here at American Instruments," Jim added with a sly smile.

"Hold on," Bert said. "What's this have to do with economic forecasting? That's where we started, remember?"

"According to Big Bucks," Harry replied, "just about everybody in the States has two cars, two TV sets, and at least one of every appliance. So who's left to buy? The people overseas aren't going to buy from us, when they can buy it cheaper in Japan."

"Hmm," Bert said, impressed. "He's put his finger on the heart of the matter. A little simplistic, but right on target." He glanced at his shoes, thinking that he needed a shine.

The three men walked out to the elevator.

"How'd you make out?" Bert asked his secretary as he walked into her cubicle. He glanced at the bright picture post cards from around the world that covered one wall.

"Not too badly, just had to retype the first few pages. How about you?" She glanced at the rain coat folded over the stain.

"No problem. By the way, did you know that the shoe shine man was called Daddy Big Bucks?"

"Who, Hiawatha? Well that depends. Some of the secretaries who have gotten flowers and candy from him call him *Sweet* Daddy Big Bucks."

"What do you call him?" Bert asked.

"I'm over twenty-five," she said with a grin, and turned back to her typing.

"Send him in the next time he comes," Bert called over his shoulder as he walked into his office, reading the report, missing the huge smile that spread over Bridget's face.

CHAPTER TWO

"It's Daddy," Bridget announced.

"Who?" Bert barked into the phone. His father had been dead for ten years; besides, he could never imagine calling his straightlaced West Indian father "Daddy."

"Hiawatha Jackson, the shoe shine man."

"Oh, right, send him in." Bert began to smile as he recalled the scene in the cafeteria the week before. He looked up to see the wizened face staring at him from the doorway. He had on a blue smock over a buttoned-down light brown shirt with a subtle stripe and a matching paisley tie. The bright lights reflected off his cuff links. He leaned to the left, favoring the hand that held the portable shoe shine stand the size of a large bread box on which stood a black metal foot stand. It was made of light pine and had a high gloss.

"Understand you finally want a shine?" He eyed Bert suspiciously.

"Come in, come in—how are you today?"

Big Bucks ignored the question and walked slowly across the room and around to where Bert was sitting behind his desk, lowered his box to the floor, and squatted, his small bony butt a few inches off the floor. Suddenly there was a loud report from the shoe shine box. Bert, who had been glancing at a magazine, looked up in alarm just in time to see the bolt on the box retract into its mounting, and the top of the box, including the metal stand, slowly rise, revealing an interior lined with black suede and divided into a number of compartments. One contained a folded *Wall Street Journal*; the others, boxes and jars of what looked like samples. A strong odor of perfume and soap rose from the box.

"High tech," explained Big Bucks with a touch of pride as he extracted a battered tin of black polish, a dirty rag, and an ancient brush, the bristles concave with wear. With one finger and a little smile he closed the box.

"Gettin' a little old, feelin' a little tired," he said, placing Bert's foot firmly on the stand.

"Beg pardon?"

"You asked how I was feelin'," Big Bucks said in a miffed tone.

"Oh yeah."

"Goddamn, that's big," the old man exclaimed, examining the big black wingtip shoe. "Close to fifteen, I'd say."

"Thirteen," Bert snapped defensively.

"Should charge you extra," Daddy muttered half to himself. "What kind of shine you want, deluxe or regular?"

"What's the difference?"

"Regular's two dollars, deluxe's three—high class man like you better take deluxe."

"I'll take regular," Bert announced, determined not to be buffaloed. When the old man opened the tin, Bert could

11

see there was only a ring of black polish around the bottom. Big Bucks passed the rag hurriedly over it. He then ran the rag over the shoe, the old shine clearly visible through the film of freshly applied polish.

"Understand you have a pretty good grasp of what's going on in the economy?"

"Who you been talkin' to?" Big Bucks asked, a suspicious look on his face.

"Jim and Harry."

"Oh, them." He sat back on his haunches and leisurely stroked the shoes.

"Well, you know, I talks to all the big boys 'round here. Hell, when am shinin' the Chairman's shoes we always has us a long talk." He looked closely at Bert's shoe and shook his head.

"About what?"

"We talks economics. Matter of fact, I were in shinin' Ellman's shoes a couple of weeks ago, told him, then, unemployment was gonna pass ten percent."

"Abe?"

"That's right," the gnome said belligerently.

"What did he say to that?" Bert asked, gleefully imagining this scene between the pompous Comptroller and Big Bucks. He knew that Abe would rather die than own up to discussing the economy with a shoe shine man.

"Hell, he showed me a whole bunch of charts and figures to prove unemployment wouldn't go over eight percent. I say to him, 'I don't care how many figures you shows me. I read the *Journal* and I know what's happenin' in the street and I'm sayin' to you right now, unemployment is goin' to ten percent, maybe more.' Then he tell me he got fifty bucks that say it won't. Goddamn it, don't you know, one week later it hit ten percent."

"What did Abe say?" Bert asked with a grin.

Big Bucks stopped any pretense of brushing. "Went by his office to collect. His secretary say he was out. Sh-e-e-e-t.

I knew he was in there. He just couldn't face me because I won. Caught him one night when his wife was in the office, shamed him into payin' me."

"How'd you know it was going that high—a lucky guess?"

"Guess, my ass," Big Bucks snorted, his eyes opened wide. "Hell it ain't that difficult to see, if you keeps your eyes open and talks to people. America's in a lot of trouble, economic-wise. As I see it, ain't nobody gonna buy from us when they can get cheaper and better over in Japan."

"Come on now," teased Bert, "did you think it up yourself? Sounds like something the Chairman would say."

"Chairman didn't tell me shit. I ain't no fool, you know. You sit up here in your three-piece suit with the tight pants and think you know something. I told the Chairman just what I told you."

Big Bucks by this time was standing in front of Bert's desk as he talked and gestured, the bottom of his blue smock jumping in response to his jerky body movements. He followed Bert's eyes to his shoes, hurriedly moved back to his box, and slid the other shoe on the stand, giving it two passes with the brush.

"Chairman old Navy man like me," he continued from his squatting position, "but 'fraid he losin' his grip, lettin' too many things get by him."

"I'm sure he hangs on your every word," Bert responded sarcastically.

"He listen alright—just don't do nothin'. That'll be two bucks," he announced, standing up straight. "I know you ain't used to gettin' shines, but I generally gets a buck tip."

Without thinking, Bert fished three dollars out and gave them to Big Bucks, who, with a practiced motion, added them to the mammoth roll of bills he'd pulled from his pants pocket.

"Don't ask for no tip on deluxe."

13

Bert stood and stared at him in disbelief.

"Tried to get you to take deluxe."

Bert looked down at his shoes. "That's not much of a shine for three bucks."

"Shouldn't wait so long between shines," Big Bucks muttered, and was out the door.

Bert got up, stretched his long frame, and looked out the window on to Battery Park. He saw an oil tanker pass lying low in the water.

"Not much difference," Bridget commented, standing beside him, the mail in her hand, and looking down at his shoes. Her eyes came up to meet his that were fixed on her bosom. Self-conscious under his stare, she adjusted her blouse and busied herself around the desk.

"It cost me three bucks. Remind me to call Harry tomorrow, I want to talk to him about that bandit."

CHAPTER THREE

"You'll be late for the meeting," Bridget said from the doorway. "By the way, don't forget you wanted to talk to Harry about Sweet Daddy Big Bucks." She had an impish grin on her face.

"Hmm, so it's Sweet Daddy now?" Bert asked, looking at her as he took the file she held out to him.

The meeting in Harry's office had been called to choose a minority employee to represent the company on Minority Youth Day at City Hall.

The meeting had already started when Bert arrived. He was greeted by a heavy sweet scent, as he joined the five other executives. Harry's office boasted the only white bearskin rug in the company. He had only recently been transferred from Los Angeles and still wore bright-colored suits, much to his boss's chagrin. Bert strode over the white rug as if it wasn't there. Harry shot him a sour grimace from his desk. The only empty seat was across from the wall that was lined with three rows of awards and plaques. Bert sat down and focused on the flip chart beside Harry's desk that contained six names and, on the seventh line, in bold letters, the initials **D.B.B.**

"Sorry to start without you," Harry said, looking directly at Bert.

"That's okay," Bert responded as he flipped rapidly through his file. "I'm familiar with the first six names, but what's the initials for?"

"Daddy Big Bucks," Harry answered, his face turning red.

Several members of the committee looked around, embarrassed.

"Come on," exclaimed Bert. "You've got to be kidding. He doesn't even work for the company."

"I know. We're just brainstorming," Harry said, "but I gotta say, if I had my way he'd be the guy I'd send out to talk to minority students. At least they could relate to him."

"I'll drink to that," Jim blurted out from the corner.

After the meeting broke up, Bert said, looking at the pair, "That guy's a real bandit. What kind of example is that for young kids?"

"He doesn't think too highly of you either," Harry retorted. "The way he put it was that you were just 'another one of those tightwads, too cheap to get a deluxe shine'— said he didn't bother trying to sell you any Watkins products."

"Hell with him," Bert snorted.

"Careful," Jim said. "Understand he and the Chairman had quite a talk about you." Harry straightened out the white bearskin rug with the tip of his highly shined shoe.

"About me?" Bert asked, a smile of disbelief breaking out on his face.

"Why, sure," Jim replied, getting up from his seat. "Where do you think we get all our poop?"

"Him? Aw, I can't believe that."

"Why not?" asked Jim. "He makes it a practice to shine the Chairman's shoes right after the Board meeting."

"You guys are serious," Bert said in awe.

"If you want to know what the Chairman is thinking, you'd better get in Big Bucks' confidence," Jim continued, walking to the door.

Bert, following him, shook his head, and muttered, "I'll be damned."

"You're gonna have to buy Watkins products from him if you expect him to give any information," Jim added. "I'd suggest laundry soap."

"Or room freshener," Harry interjected, standing in the doorway. "That's what you smell in here—can't stand it myself, but I always use it around Board meeting time."

"Okay," said Bert, leaving Harry's office. "Ask him to stop up."

"Don't forget laundry soap," Harry called after him.

It was late in the afternoon when Hiawatha Jackson appeared in the doorway with something that could almost pass for a smile on his face, the gold in his teeth flashing. "Hear you interested in buying some product?"

"Yeah," the younger man replied, getting up from his desk. The two men met at Bert's coffee table, above which hung a picture of the golden shrine at Kyoto. Big Bucks lowered his shoe shine box onto the highly polished surface of the table. Bert started to object, but thought better of it. They both waited for the click of the high tech bolt, the top rising to reveal sample boxes lined up neatly. Big Bucks deftly picked out two boxes, one can, and a bottle, and lined them up on the table with the brown and white Watkins labels facing the same direction.

"Now, this is real soap," Big Bucks declared. "Not that weak shit you buy in the supermarket."

17

"I always thought soap was soap."

"Sh-e-e-e-t, that's what they get you to believe. They pay so much for the advertisement they cain't afford to put power in."

"I see."

"Damn right. Now, this is so powerful"—he held it out to Bert to smell—"your wife's only have to wash oncet a month."

Bert recoiled from the strong smell of ammonia.

"You gets used to it," Big Bucks assured him, capping the can. He returned it to the line of samples and picked up a bottle. Just then, Bridget entered, deposited mail in Bert's box, and laid out two memos on his desk.

"How'd you like that polish?" Big Bucks asked her.

"Fine, just fine."

"Sold her some of this here furniture polish last week," Daddy said, holding up the bottle. "Come with a year's guarantee." There was real pride in his voice.

"I really liked it," Bridget confirmed.

Big Bucks beamed.

"I'll take a case of laundry soap," Bert concluded, walking over to his desk, as Big Bucks pulled out his order pad and began to write.

Bridget said, "Good night."

Putting the pad away, the old man picked up his box and moved over to Bert, the sweet scent of samples still in the air.

"Hear you and the Chairman been discussing me," Bert said nonchalantly.

"Who told you that?"

"Some friends," Bert said, feeling he'd bought the soap for nothing.

"Well, I'll tell you, I'm very careful who I tell things to. You be my steady customer and we get to know each other, why, from time to time I'll let you in on a little sumpin'."

Only the hum of the flourescent lights could be heard over the sound of the shoe brush.

"How'd you get in this business anyway?"

Big Bucks gave a little grin and straightened up.

Heartened by the look, Bert added, "I never thought anybody could make money shining shoes."

Big Bucks snorted. "That's what most folks think. A lot of 'em looks down on me, but I don't care—I can buy and sell most of 'em,"

"Guess you've been shinin' shoes all your life?"

"Hell, naw," Big Bucks said, leaning back on the credenza, "I used to be a typesetter. Worked out at Allied Press back in the '50s."

"Allied Press? Out in Jersey?"

"Only one Allied Press," the little man replied with a wry grin.

Ah ha, thought Bert, I've caught the little bastard now. He knew Allied Press had only hired skilled typesetters and never Colored, as they were called in those days. Moving in for the kill, he asked, "How'd you get a job like that?"

Big Bucks pulled a toothpick out of his shirt pocket, started chewing it, and said, "Come out of Cleveland—used to work for Gatwick Brothers. That's where I learned to be a typesetter. Came East to visit my brother. One day I decided to get in on big business. They was payin' lots of overtime. I knew it wasn't gonna be easy—happened to know a guy who used to drive for my Senator. Got me a letter from the Senator's office recommendin' me. Went to work the next day. Only jigaboo in the whole damn section. Foreman tried to mess with me at first, but I straightened his ass out. Then, when he found out what a good worker I was, we became good friends. 'Course it got a little troublesome tryin' to keep him and the union happy." He ended with a little sheepish smile.

19

"That's impossible," Bert said with a scoff. "I used to be a time study engineer."

"One of them, huh? Well, let me tell you, I used to bust that rate all the time. That's why the foreman loved me."

"I'll bet the union didn't love you."

"Couldn't never prove nothin'. Foreman always covered up. Besides, every time the shop steward started up, I'd ask him if he'd ever seen a Colored man that wasn't for the union. That used to shut him up."

Bert shook his head in amused silence, then said, "How in the hell did you get into this business?"

"Plain old luck."

"Luck?"

"Yeah. Happened to be visitin' a buddy down at the Bixbey Buildin'—you know, down on Water Street?"

The younger man shook his head.

"Well, anyway," Big Bucks said, moving the toothpick to the other side of his mouth, "got to talkin' to this Eyetalyan fellow, waitin' for my buddy, said he was too old to keep shinin' shoes, wanted to sell out. Well, soon as he told me he put four children through college, I knew that was the business for me. So I just used that overtime money to buy him out, then scouted 'round lookin' for where the oldest shoe shine men were at, and slipped the buildin' super a little somethin' to let me know when they kicked off, so I could pick up the franchise." He paused, chewed on the toothpick, and indulged himself in a satisfied smile. "After that," he continued, "decided to get into real estate. Bought me some old houses real cheap."

Realizing he had greatly underestimated this man, Bert asked, "So you were brought up in Cleveland?"

"Naw, Mississippi," the old man responded, gathering up his polish and brushes. "Came up when I was six-

teen. Didn't want no more part of that place. Caught me a
freight train out at three o'clock in the mornin'."

"Somebody chasing you?"

"Worse than that." Big Bucks' face suddenly took on
a grim fearful look, his eyes staring out into the distance:
The silent office seemed to echo the croaking quality that
entered his voice. "Couldn't believe what that place was
like," he murmured half to himself. He seemed to slip into
a trance right before Bert's eyes. "It was bad. Took off school
one mornin'—was gonna do a little huntin'—come into the
clearin' and bumped right into it before I saw it. Then the
wind shifted and the stink almost knocked me over. Must
have been there three days. We'd all thought he'd be out
drunk somewhere, like he usually do. Could see where
they cut his dick off. Flies on him rose up like a cloud when
I cut him down. Knew I have to get the fuck out of there."

"Did you know him?" Bert asked gently.

"My Daddy," Big Bucks croaked, turning his face
away to hide the tears, and walked swiftly out, his foot-
steps sounding clearly in the empty corridor.

Bert sat staring into space, thinking about it.

Four hours later, Bert got off the elevator on the elev-
enth floor of his apartment building. He opened the door
leading out to the open hallway and, looking out over the
West Side of Manhattan, shook his head, wondering how
he had ever let Dotty talk him into the co-op. Bunch of nuts,
he thought, to design a building with an outside hallway.
It had scared the living hell out of him the first time he saw
the place. "I'm home," he called as the wind slammed the
door shut behind him.

"That you, sweety?" Dotty called from the kitchen.
"Dinner's almost ready."

"Hi," he answered, and walked past the kitchen to the living room, one side of which was a huge picture window that looked down on Columbus Avenue and out to Central Park. He dropped his briefcase beside the heavy black leather chair, picked up the mail, leafed through it, and put it back down on the side table. Bert carefully picked his way around the glass coffee table on which stood two Ibeji sculptures, and followed the delicious aroma into the kitchen, where Dotty stood over the stove, her soft dark brown arms contrasting with her nurse's uniform. She absently patted her close-cut Afro that wreathed her pretty round face, and added spices to a pot. Bert came up behind her, studying how her nurse's uniform showed off her figure, and grabbed her with both hands.

"Don't be foolin' with me when I'm cooking," she said angrily, stirring the golden brown rice and meat dish. Dotty, who was a full foot shorter than Bert, still maintained the petite figure that had won her the title of Miss Harlem many more years before than she liked to remember.

"Damn, you don't have to get mad."

"I'm sorry." Her voice softened perceptibly, she turned, reached up, and kissed her husband. "I know you're gonna like this. What's a matter with you?" she asked, handing him a bowl of food. "Besides, what you doing coming home so late—better not be some other chick."

"Ah, come on Dotty. It was this guy at work. Told me a very sad story," Bert replied, as they sat down to the table.

"Since when did you start feelin' sorry for anyone around American Instruments?"

"He doesn't work there, he's the shoe shine man."

"Now you feelin' sorry for the shoe shine man. Is that the same cat that clipped you for three dollars last week?

22

He ought to be feelin' sorry for you." The smell of fried plantains hovered over the table when Dotty uncovered the bowl.

"You don't understand. His father was lynched."

"When?" she asked, picking up Bert's plate to serve him.

"Oh, a long time ago. He was just telling me today."

"How come?"

"Well, I had ordered some Watkins soap, and he began telling me about—"

"Watkins soap!" Dotty exclaimed. "That smelly crap? That's all we could afford in Harlem. I promised myself I'd never smell that mess again. Ammonia stays in your skin forever."

"It was only a case."

"Damn, Bert, you West Indians kill me. Y'all supposed to be so smart, yet some half slick nigger from Harlem comes down there and takes three dollars for a shine you never got, and now he's about to unload some of that foul-smellin' Watkins junk on you. You need to have grown up in Harlem. I learned to spot them types when I was six years old."

"Well, he's in with the Chairman," Bert muttered.

"In with the *Chairman*? He shine shoes too?"

"Forget it," Bert snapped.

"Well, I've got duty tonight. Do the dishes, will you, hon?" Dotty pecked him on the cheek.

"Okay. I got that co-op board meeting."

"Good luck with the kooks," Dotty grinned as she walked out the door.

CHAPTER FOUR

Several weeks later, Big Bucks suddenly popped into Bert's office late one afternoon.

"Understand you've been travelin'," he said from the doorway.

"Yeah," Bert said proudly. "In Europe. Come in."

"I can see," the old man replied, walking over to Bert's desk and looking at his shoes. "Them people don't believe in shinin' shoes, except Eyetalyans."

"I didn't know you'd been in Europe."

"In the Navy—traveled all over." Big Bucks eased his shoe box to the floor. "How your wife like that soap?"

"Not too well. She comes from Harlem."

The old man let out a small embarrassed grunt, put another coat of polish on, and, after a pause said, "Maybe you ought to try the room freshener. That's bound to please her."

"I was wondering," Bert said firmly, "what the Chairman thought about my speech."

The silence that followed was interrupted only by the squeal of polish being rubbed into leather. "You gettin' a good shine today," Daddy muttered, ignoring the younger man's question.

The lanky executive stared down at the shiny processed hair in silence, and was about to repeat his question when the phone rang.

"It's Harry," Bridget announced.

"Big Bucks been looking for you," Harry exclaimed. "Did you ever find out what the Chairman said about you?"

"No," Bert replied, watching the old man still bent over his shoes, raised his voice, and added, "I don't know what the Chairman thinks, but I'm not buying any more soap till I find out. I'm busy now. I'll call you later."

"Been meanin' to tell you," Daddy murmured, peering up. "The Chairman said you did pretty good at the Board meeting."

Bert repressed his smile of victory.

"What's Harry sayin' about me? Still claimin' I don't hire my own people?"

"Do you?" asked Bert, still flushed.

"Now, he don't know what he's talkin' about. I got two of my cousins workin' for me—couple of sorry bastards."

"How come they were gettin' on your case?"

"Jim knew I wasn't serious about not hirin' Blacks— what I said was, 'Black folks don't want to work when it comes to a piddlin' job like shinin' shoes.' Harry gits all excited. Worst thing in the world, White liberals. Where the hell was he when I needed a job?"

"I can't imagine you ever needing a job."

"You right, because I have my own business."

"Yeah, but can't you understand, it wasn't that long ago we couldn't do anything *but* shine shoes?" Bert asked, looking down at his own, which had the closest thing to a gleam since Big Bucks had started shining them.

"Goddamn Eastern Europeans work like hell—I go around on Monday mornin', got my twenty dollars sittin' there waitin' for me. Get to my cousins, them bastards always got some damn excuse."

"Yeah, but don't you think you've got a responsibility to hire our people? After all, if you don't, who will?"

"Not if they ain't gonna work, I won't. Since you feel so strong 'bout it, why don't you git out, start a business, hire as many people as you want? Anybody workin' for me gotta hustle like me." The old man rose from his crouch and walked around the office. "Gotta work them kinks out," he said, massaging one thigh. "Keepin' in shape for my womens," he added with a sly grin.

"You're a hard man, Big Bucks. You sound like a Reagan Republican."

"Naw, naw, I ain't no Republican. Fact is I don't care for the whole lot of 'em," the gnome replied. He approached the window and looked out on Battery Park.

"Who?"

"All politicians."

"How about your Senator?"

"He was different, God rest his soul."

"I suppose the next thing you'll tell me is that Blacks should pull themselves up by their bootstraps, huh?" Bert asked, with more than a hint of anger in his voice.

"I'll tell you this," the shoe shine man retorted, turning and looking at the thin man shrewdly, "Reagan is the best thing that ever happened to Black folks."

"What?" Bert exploded. His foot slid off the stand and smacked the floor. Bridget stuck her head in the office, glanced around quizzically, and, seeing that nothing disastrous had happened, closed the door.

"That sure is a whole lot of woman," the shoe shine man commented.

"She's over twenty-five," the executive sarcastically replied.

"I'll tell you one thing," Big Bucks continued. "Reagan got niggers off they ass, made 'em take a holt of things, didn't he?"

Bert's face flushed. "Next you're going to tell me that the Civil Rights Movement was a big mistake, huh? Let me warn you, I was in the Movement, and it was the greatest thing that ever happened." Bert realized he could be heard through the closed door, but he didn't give a damn.

"Now you said all that," Big Bucks responded soothingly, "I didn't. If you'd lived in the South like I did, you'd know what the civil rights thing meant to me. Why, it's a miracle to go back down there and see how them crackers is actin' like they done changed their ways. But that ain't what I'm sayin'."

Bert stared at the older man, unconvinced.

Big Bucks, who had been leaning on Bert's credenza, slid his butt up on it, his short legs dangling, a pair of calf-length black socks separating his tailored pants from his gleaming shoes.

"Well, the way I see it, the Movement was doin' all right while King was runnin' it. Then ole Lyndon jumped into the act and made it all into a poverty program. Hell, that wasn't what Black folks was fightin' for—we was fightin' for equal rights."

"Well, he was only trying to help Blacks."

"Sh-e-e-e-t. Government began throwin' out money every which way, got the young folks believin' that's the way it's supposed to be. Older folks, should have knowed better, just sat there and let them think that White folks really loved 'em and was gonna keep on givin' 'em money. Young nephew of mine graduated in Accounting, got a job with General Foods—don't you know he turned right around and took a job with one of them antipoverty programs, 'cause they offered more money? I asked him, 'How you gonna learn to keep up with the White boys, sittin' up in this backwater?'" An agitated look spread over Daddy's face.

"What did he say to that?"

"Gave me some jackass answer. Last month they cut off the funds. Come askin' to borrow some money."

"Did you loan him any?" Bert asked, knowing the answer.

"Shit, naw, the sorry bastard," he said, swinging his short legs. "Offered him a shine stand—make more than he did as an accountant."

"What happened?"

"Looked at me like I was crazy."

Bert smiled, imagining the scene. "Yeah, but that's just one example. Those programs brought real jobs into the ghetto."

"*Weren't* no real jobs!" Bucks shouted indignantly, his hand gripping the top of the credenza. "Ain't no average man gonna pay real money for what they was doin'. You know as well as I do that it was the White man's way of shuttin' niggers up—see how quickly they shut it off, don't you?"

Bert was silent.

"You ain't got no answer to that, do you?" Daddy asked, glaring.

Bridget buzzed. "It's Dotty, on line three."

"Excuse me," Bert said to the little man, "it's my wife. Hi, dear."

"Hi, sweety. Sorry to bother you, but Henry's called four times and I didn't want to give him your office number."

"What now?" Bert asked with a sigh.

"Problems with the super, I gather—I didn't ask."

"I'll call him. God, you'd think he could handle some of these things. He's the President."

"Henry's not gonna solve any problems as long as he has you on the Governing Board."

"Got to go, dear."

"Busy?"

"I was talking to Big Bucks."

"Who?"

"The shoe shine guy." He looked up and saw the gnome staring at a painting.

"Them folks payin' you to talk to the shoe shine man?"

"Goodbye, Dotty."

"Home regular time?"

"Yep."

"What's this?" Big Bucks demanded, indicating the large painting with a metallic gold frame, hanging next to the window.

"An African king," the tall executive responded, leaning back in his chair.

The old man looked puzzled.

"It's the sculpture of a Benin king. The original is in the London Museum."

"Ugly sonofabitch, ain't he?"

"That's an art style. You just don't understand African art."

"I know ugly when I see it—what's it doin' in London?"

"They stole it when they ruled Nigeria."

"Must be valuable."

29

"It's worth about three million."

"What? You shittin' me?"

"Think I'm kidding, call the Metropolitan Museum."

The old man looked at the painting from a different angle.

"Not so ugly anymore?" Bert taunted, getting up to stretch his legs.

"How you learn about this?" the old man asked, standing over Bert's desk.

"My wife—it's her hobby."

"Y'all own any?"

"A few pieces. Tripled in value since we bought them."

Surprise registered in Daddy's eyes. "No shit?"

"No shit."

"Imagine that," the old man said, examining the painting from another angle.

"Well," Bert went on, "I still don't agree with you about Johnson. I think he was morally committed to rectifying old wrongs."

"Huh?"

"Lyndon Johnson, remember?"

"Oh, yeah," Daddy said, moving back to the desk. "I don't quarrel with you on that—wasn't so much what he did, as to the way people looked at it. First place, Black folks got to thinkin' that, as long they were mixed in with poverty, White folks would finally give 'em a break. Didn't realize that White folks don't like poor folks no more than they do niggers. In fact, now that some of us got little money, we actin' the same way. On top of that, Black people got to listenin' to what a few liberal big mouths was sayin', that all White folks had changed. That was all right as long as everything was goin' on right, economic-wise. But now that Japan and other countries is takin' our trade, goddamn money got cut off—ain't gonna be turned back on either, let me tell you."

A sudden knock on the door jolted Bert upright in his seat, and the older man slid off the credenza.

"The Chairman's office called," Bridget told him in a business-like voice. "They want to see you now."

"We'll finish this later," Bert said.

"That'll be three dollars *now*," Big Bucks demanded, trailing the executive out of the door.

The usual quietness of the executive floor was shattered, as the executives spilled out of the Chairman's office. Bert caught up with Jim as they neared the receptionist's desk.

"Going to lunch?"

"Yes," Jim replied, "but let's go out. I can't take that cafeteria more than once a week." He held the elevator door for Bert, who had been shoved back, as Dibble, the head of Legal, pushed his bulk onto the elevator.

Bert glared at Dibble, who was deep in conversation with Buckminister, the Chairman's assistant.

"Insensitive bastard," Bert growled, as the elevator emptied in the lobby.

"Who?" Jim asked, carefully putting on his dark glasses.

"Dibble. He reminds me of another self-centered bugger, Big Bucks."

"Oh, how?" Jim preceded the taller man through the revolving door, into the hot, humid air of Wall Street, and they threaded their way north on Nassau Street, through the midday crowd.

"The bastard attacks everything near and dear to me."

"Oh, he'll do that all right—want to try here?" Jim indicated a small Italian restaurant with bright red curtains in the window.

The smell of cooking pasta and garlic filled the crowded little room. Waitresses with white blouses and long black

31

skirts sped up and down the narrow aisle. People from the nearest table stared at the couple—one barely five feet, the other over six and a half.

"He says what's on his mind, and, since he's his own boss he can get away with it," Jim said, as they were seated.

"Yeah, well, he can't go around saying things like that." Bert snorted and spread butter on a slice of bread—"Try some of this, it's hot."

"He's antagonistic by nature, but, you gotta admit, he's saying a lot of things we *think* but don't *dare* say."

"Like what?" Bert spat out.

"Take his favorite topic," Jim said, lifting a buttered crust to his mouth. "That Reagan will get Black folks off their asses."

"That's what he was pushing this morning."

Both men were silent as Jim swallowed his mouthful. Then he said, "Unfortunately, he gets peoples hackles up so fast that they never hear the rest of his thesis—that Black folks have *always* made their own way, and always under great odds. That's why he claims the war on poverty was an unfortunate detour on the road to progress."

"What in the hell is his answer?" Bert demanded, looking up at the attractive waitress who stood over their table.

"Now, that's Big Bucks' type," Jim grinned as they watched the receding long-skirted waitress swish her way back to the kitchen.

"You haven't answered my question," the tall man reminded.

"His main gripe seems to be there are no Black businessmen to speak of. And, as he puts it, all the younger generation wants to do is get into a big corporation and go to sleep."

"I wish him luck, there never have been any real Black businesses, except in the South, and that got blown away after integration."

"He happens to see this as a very serious problem, in fact I hear he's financed several businesses in Harlem."

"Are we talking about the same man?" Bert asked, unfolding his napkin, as the waitress brought their appetizers.

"He's a complex character, he feels very strongly that until we have more Black business, we'll continue to have high unemployment and poverty. I hasten to add, however, it wasn't all altruism."

"How so?"

"Well the case I'm familiar with, was when he loaned money to a restaurant owner who was going broke. The first week Bucks forced the man to fire all of his relatives, even his wife."

"You're kidding."

"Wait, next he makes him sell his new Cadillac, but at the end of three months, the business was making money."

"I'm sure," Bert said with a big grin, "the guy paid dearly for the loan."

"No doubt, but, the guy's still in business."

"If he *really* puts his money where his mouth is, I'm impressed."

They finished eating in silence. As they were splitting the check, Jim asked, "By the way, did he tell you what the Chairman thought of your speech?"

"Yeah, I finally dragged it out of him. Cost me a case of soap and a box of deluxe room freshener, not to mention shoe shines."

"He doesn't come cheap," Jim commented as they left the restaurant.

CHAPTER FIVE

Bridget walked in with a brisk stride. She was wearing her honey-blonde hair upswept, her tight fitting blue skirt clashed with her red stockings, and an ivory brooch held the collar of the white blouse close to her neck. As she sat opposite her boss she noticed his look of disappointment when he eyed her bosom in the no-nonsense blouse. It was Monday, the day she usually wore a low-cut blouse, to, as she thought of it, give the office a lift. It alone, she discovered, could bring Bert's droopy eyes to full alertness that early in the week. She opened the notebook that lay in her lap, ready for dictation.

"By the way, a case of room freshener came for you. I put it in your closet," she said, tucking in a wisp of hair.

"Thanks," he mumbled. "I don't dare send it home."

"Why? It's not that bad. I use it myself."

"Dotty's from Harlem. They used it all the time."

"I know how that is," she said with a deep sigh.

"I feel like a damn fool. I don't know why I keep buying his stuff. The inside poop he gets from the Chairman's office isn't that great."

34

Bridget smiled. "I see he's really getting to you," she said, closing her notebook and settling back in her chair.

"He's weird. You should hear some of the crap he tells me."

"Really? I think he's rather attractive."

"Attractive? You've got to be kidding."

"No," she said firmly. "He may not fit the corporate mold, but he's sure carved out a career for himself."

"Hah. You call that a career, shining shoes?"

"He's in real estate too," she said defensively.

"Probably sucking the blood out of tenants in some slum."

"Well, at least he can do what he wants. He doesn't have to depend on a corporation for *everything*."

"Neither do I."

"Oh, come on, Mr. Davis. You go to the airport by company limousine, they tell you how much you can spend for expenses—that can all disappear overnight, you know. Listen, I come from a poor Irish family, and I learned early in life that the only thing you could be sure of is what *you* owned. I admire Hiawatha. He's a poor man who fought his way up."

Unable to think of a retort, Bert picked up his yellow legal pad and began to dictate.

When he returned to his office after lunch, Bridget was wearing a sly smile and motioned her head towards the office. Sure enough, there stood Big Bucks, leaning back against the credenza, reading the *Wall Street Journal*. He folded it quickly and returned it to his box as Bert strode in.

"Come to finish our talk," Hiawatha said.

"Okay by me," Bert responded, closing the door.

"Well now, it appears I shocked you yesterday," Daddy began, a wide grin breaking out on his prune-like face.

"Frankly, I've never heard a Black man talk like that."

35

"Am I lyin'?" There was a certain belligerence in his voice.

"Damnit, it's the way you say things."

The smile still played around Daddy's wrinkled lips. "You younger cats is too much. Here you are, tryin' to be White, yet, when I don't think about Black people the way you do, I'm wrong." He made no move towards his kit lying on the floor.

Bert gritted his teeth and reminded himself that he would stay calm. When he brought himself under control, he said, "You lost me on that one."

"I don't see no difference between you and these White boys down here. All y'all ready to kill each other to get as close to the top as you can."

"What do you suggest, I take over one of your shine stands?" the tall man snapped.

"Nothin' wrong with what you doin'. Fact is, I admire you. Wisht I had some education. It's jes that you and Jim act like you the only ones who knows what's good for *all* Black people. Y'all's shit stinks jes like everybody else's."

"Look," roared Bert, "I did my time in the trenches. I marched with King in Montgomery and in Mississippi. I'm a product of that dream. I'm opening the way for others to follow." He waited to see what impact his declaration would have on the old man.

Big Bucks fished out a toothpick, slipped it into his mouth, and began to chew. "Trouble is, time done passed you by, just like them big guns in the civil rights."

Bert slid into his seat, leaving the older man standing, and waited for him to continue.

Hiawatha shifted to the other foot, and leaned back on the bookcase. "But shit," he said in exasperation, "twenty years done passed since the Civil Rights Movement and they still got the same old people in charge. You and Jim are the same way. Your ideas about Black folks is twenty years old—y'all still think the answer is to be a doctor or lawyer 'stead of makin' some real money, even if it means you gets a little dirty.''

Bert shook his head in amused silence. His ideas had been called many things, but never twenty years old.

''What I'm sayin' is, bein' an example to young folks don't mean much if all the jobs go to Japan.''

''Who said they're all going to Japan?''

''Your report. It was lyin' right there on the Chairman's desk.''

Bert Davis smiled in spite of himself.

The old man shifted his stance and continued, ''You know our product's too expensive for the rest of the world. Companies can't afford to keep peoples who don't do nothin' but tell other people what to do.''

''What are you saying?'' asked the younger man, squirming uncomfortably in his seat. ''That I'm going to lose my job?''

''See what happened in Detroit, don't you?'' The gnome stood right over Bert. ''My buddy, Shorty, worked at one of them GM plants, makin' thirty-five dollars an hour plus overtime. I told him, 'You jes kiddin' yourself if you think this gonna last. Damn Japs only gettin' ten dollars an hour and makin' good cars, y'all turnin' out crap.' You seen some of that shit Detroit been puttin' out.''

''I can't argue with you there, but—''

''See what happened when the recession hit, didn't you? Went through Detroit like shit through a goose.''

''Yeah, the future doesn't look too great,'' Bert admitted.

''That's my point. If White folks in for a bad time, you know what's gonna happen to us.''

Bert stared at the shoe shine man, saying nothing, but deep in thought.

"Ain't but one thing gonna help Black folks, that's havin' our own business. Malcolm tried to tell us that, but wasn't many of us listenin'." The gnarled old man's eyes took on a misty look. "Never forget that man long as I live. Went up and spoke to him oncet after a meetin', told him I was a typesetter. Man, don't you know he looked down on me and say, 'Brother, we needs people like you who understand production.' That's what he said. Couldn't see his eyes on account of his shades, but a chill come over me. Never felt nothin' like that before or since." The old man stared out the window as if he were in a different time and place.

Bert followed Big Bucks' stare, and his mind moved back in time. "Yeah, I heard him at the 369th Armory once, cops all over the place, all the Muslim men in dark blue suits and almost bald heads, the women with long gowns. I was a time study engineer at the time, and I got that same feeling when he said Black people had to learn all about production. It was the first time that anyone of my race seemed to understand what I was trying to do. My family thought I was a fool not to go to medical school. In fact, that's where I met my wife Dotty." A smile crossed his face.

Big Bucks looked closely at him, and with a fragile smile said, "You figure Malcolm knew things might turn out economic-wise like they is, and was tryin' to warn us?"

"Don't know," Bert answered. "I do know all the experts are saying that any future growth will come from small business."

"Hell, yeah," the shoe shine man said, leaving his post by the window. "It's been what I've been tryin' to tell you. You been to Harlem lately? Goddamn boat people done come ashore.''

"Huh?''

"You ain't seen them fruit stores?''

"Oh, you mean the Koreans? They're not boat people.''

"Oh yeah? Seen how they come in and take over?''

"They just saw an opportunity and took it.''

"Oh, I ain't downin' 'em. Fact is I admire 'em. Whole damn family works. What gits me is that we whipped the Japs in war and they come over here and do better than us. Spanish come up from Puerto Rica, got them bodegas all over the place. Now here come the boat people, takin' over right in the middle of Harlem.''

"Koreans, not boat people,'' Bert insisted.

"Don't make no never mind. All I know is that everybody done left us far behind. You educated—why you think that is?''

The tall executive was taken aback by the sudden flattery. Finally he responded, "I read where one Black economist explained that it's our slave mentality.''

"Say what?''

"He claims that because of our slave background we resent waiting on other people, and because of that we don't do very well at restaurants and other service businesses.''

"Slavery's been over for hunnert years,'' Daddy snapped.

"I'm just telling you what he said. He claims that the West Indians, on the other hand, who had a history of being in their own businesses in their own country, are quite successful here in America.''

"You West Indian, ain't ya?'' the old man asked.

"Well, yes—my father was—but that has nothing to do with it."

"Gettin' late," Big Bucks said, moving towards his shine kit. "Got some people waitin' for me."

"Which way you going?" Bert asked, "I'm leaving myself."

"Goin' to Mickall's. That's where I hangs out during the week."

"Hell, that's just a block from my apartment."

"I'll ride you up," Daddy said.

"You park down here all day?"

"Naw—peoples pick me up," Daddy explained as the taller man closed his attache case. When they passed Bridget's desk he saw her note. *Just a weird old man huh?* Bert smiled, crumpled the piece of paper, and followed Big Bucks to the elevator. "Meet out front—gotta change," the old man said, as they reached the ground floor.

"Good night, Mr. Davis," the security man said to Bert as they both stood in the glass enclosed lobby. "It's blustery out there tonight."

Before Bert could respond Big Bucks swept into view. He wore a tan camel-hair coat and a dark brown felt hat with a small red feather.

"Les go," he commanded, returning the security man's wave. The two men stepped into the cold drizzle, dodging huddled figures under umbrellas.

Hiawatha pointed to a black Mercedes Benz taking up most of the block. As they approached the car, a man of medium height, wearing a black trench coat, eased out of the driver's seat, and opened a large black umbrella against the wind.

"Evenin', Mr. Jackson," he said, as he opened the door for his boss.

"Malik, this here's one of our big executives," Daddy said by way of introduction, a note of pride in his voice.

The driver glanced at Bert, his face void of expression, and opened the front door.

"Oh, Daddy, I missed you," rose a whining, petulant voice from the rear.

"Not now, we got company," Big Bucks admonished. "Bert, this here is Cindy."

"Hi, Bert." The voice took on a low, sultry, sing-song quality.

The executive strained to get a glimpse of her, but it was too dark.

"I don't care if Bert knows I love you," her voice wailed.

The gnome gave a little laugh.

Malik's lips curled into a sneer, and he whipped the massive car away from the curb into the Wall Street traffic. In the reflection of the street lights, Bert saw that the driver was wearing a black suit and tie with his stiffly starched shirt, his eyes glued on the traffic.

"Bad night, huh?" Bert volunteered as they swung onto the West Side Drive.

Malik drove on in silence, watching the road intently. Bert looked past the driver, at the dark river.

As they emerged at 96th Street, Bucks boomed from the back seat, "You drinkin' with me." The long black Mercedes was double parked in front of Mickall's. A modern bar on the upper West Side, it featured a Gay Nineties motif and catered to the sophisticated professional types, both Black and White, from the surrounding high rise apartments. The noise of the music and the TV was deafening as the little group entered. The smell of beer mixed with perfume lent it a not unpleasant aroma. As Bert's eyes slowly

41

adjusted to the dark interior, he could see that the girl hanging on the old man's arm was very pretty. Her chocolate brown face was shaped like a heart, and she had long delicate eyelashes over dreamy eyes that seemed to drift into the distance. Below the red dress, her shapely legs ended in black pumps. She didn't look a day over twenty-five.

"Hey, Bucks," called the bartender, who wore black arm garters and sported a handlebar moustache. Several heads swung around from the nearest table. The gnome, grinning broadly, deposited his young girlfriend in the bright red dress on a bar stool, and received greetings from around the room, blowing kisses in all directions.

Bert stood silently behind the little man. The driver beside him wore a deep forbidding frown.

"Give my man here a drink," Hiawatha ordered. "I know Malik ain't gonna have one, him bein' Muslim and all."

Bert smirked to himself; another one of those Harlem hoods calling himself a Muslim.

In front of Big Bucks, the liquor bottles were stacked up three high; above them, painted on the mirror that ran the length of the bar, was a Gay Nineties dancing girl.

Bert picked up his beer, purposely held it as close as possible to the Muslim's nose, who recoiled as if he had just discovered a snake, and toasted his host. He took a mouthful, the pungent flavor of the brew stinging his throat.

Malik sniffed several times as though the very air of the room contaminated him. "Sins of the flesh," he muttered, looking at his boss.

Two men down the bar, watching television, cheered as the Mets scored a run.

"I want another," demanded the girl in red, who had been flirting with the bartender. She rubbed up against Big Bucks and ran her tongue lasciviously over her bright red lips. Bucks stood another round.

The little bar was filling up slowly. A group of four, three men and one woman, swept into the tavern laughing and joking. The woman removed her coat with a flair, shaking off the rain, and handed it to one of the men, revealing a form-fitting black dress. Her hair came down to her shoulders; her high cheekbones suggested a distinctly Oriental cast. The men watched her every move. She looked casually around the bar; then, in a lilting voice, said, "O-h-h-h-wee, it's Sweet Daddy Big Bucks," as she sauntered over to the bar.

"Disgusting," Malik growled.

She turned sideways and Bert was treated to an unimpeded view of her magnificently shaped behind.

"Looks good to me," the executive said, loud enough to reach Malik.

"Daddy," she cooed, edging up to the bar, the scent of her perfume preceding her, and pecked him on the cheek. The young girl in red's dreamy eyes grew steel-like.

"Bert," Hiawatha announced, "this here's Sugar, used to be my woman."

"Bitch," Cindy spat.

Malik's eyes were fastened on the TV set.

Ignoring the one in red, the statuesque woman cast her eyes over Bert with a slight flicker of interest, then moved back to the little man and said, "You naughty man, you haven't called me all week."

"You over twenty-five Sugar, you know that."

The noise dropped appreciably, as the whole bar waited for Sugar's response.

Her face turned scarlet.

"You got no reason to spread that lie," she said. Then flicking her head to one side, she gave him a haughty stare. "You'll be back baby, they always come back!" She sauntered back to her table, every eye in the bar riveted on her swaying rear.

43

"Goin' up my place after this," Big Bucks announced. "Gonna have womens all over the place. I seen the way Sugar looked at you—do you good to drop all that corporate shit and have some fun."

"Thanks," Bert said, "but I got a co-op meeting tonight. I'm the Treasurer."

"Where at, Columbus Towers?"

"You know it?"

"Yeah. Told you, I'm in real estate."

"Well, I've got to go," said Bert, bolting down the last of his drink.

"I'm not putting up with this," the girl in red pouted.

"Now, goddamnit Cindy, you got to realize," the old man said, "all the womens love me, they cain't help it."

Bert pulled up his coat collar.

The bartender smirked and polished a glass.

"Take me home," the girl wailed.

"Shit, bitch, ain't nobody gonna leave now."

A pained expression came over Malik's face.

Bert walked out into the rainy night.

CHAPTER SIX

It was after eight o'clock when Bert entered the meeting on the first floor of the co-op. The smell of crayons and paint hung in the air of the room, which served as a nursery during the day. The little tables and chairs were pushed back against the wall, where stick paintings in bright colors were taped to the yellow walls above them. It was filled to capacity with young professionals who refused to leave the city for the suburbs. Most of them were dressed casually—sneakers and faded jeans topped off by sweaters. Here and there were occasional suits and ties worn by older people.

Dotty, the only other Black face in the audience, waved from the rear, pointing to a seat she had saved for him.

"Where you been?" she whispered, as he sat down.

"Mickall's. What in the hell's going on?"

"Shit's hit the fan, about Caesar."

"What now?" he asked, rolling his eyes.

"Listen."

The speaker had a thick Yiddish accent. He was short and bald. "God forbid I should condemn the man—I've

45

never met him. But should we take such aggravation from a super?'' A round of clapping exploded from one side of the room. The other side glared.

"Thanks, Sol," said Henry, the Chairman, a red-headed lawyer with freckles, button eyes, and a turned-up nose, who had helped organize the co-op. "Anyone else?"

A short, plump woman with straight blonde hair and thick eyeglasses, wearing a grey warmup suit that had *Kent State* printed across the front, waved her hand furiously.

"The chair recognizes Judy Bloomstein," Henry announced.

The stout woman shot up from her seat, her hand full of papers; she peered at the opposite side of the room.

"I am damn sick and tired of people attacking Caesar. He works very hard trying to keep this building clean—"

"And fails miserably!" someone shouted from the other side.

"Come on now," Henry said, "Judy has the floor."

"I know and you know why you're trying to crucify him," the blonde woman continued. "You're all a bunch of *bigots!*" she screamed at the other side of the room.

The protests rose to a roar.

"Oh yes you are. I've watched all of you. Yes, that's what you are."

A tall, emaciated woman, wearing a yellow checkered apron over her dress, shot up from her seat. "It's obvious he didn't come down and feel *your* fanny."

Bert looked at Dotty quizzically.

Dotty nodded and whispered, "Been doing it all over the building."

"You?"

"He'd pull back half a hand," she declared, louder than she meant to.

An elderly couple turned and smiled at the Davises as if to assure them *they* weren't racists.

46

The argument continued to rage until Henry said, "All right, people—we've got to move on to other business. Bert, are you ready with the financial report?" The buzzing in the room continued.

"There's nothing new," the lanky executive reported, despite the din. "Just the same people who haven't paid their rent because we won't allow pets in the building. If we don't do something about it soon, we're going to be in default."

"Thanks, Bert," the Chairman said. "Any comments?" The two factions continued to ignore Bert's report and glare at each other as the meeting came to an end.

A stately matron with silver hair and a pince-nez, attached by a yellow ribbon to her blouse, approached Bert and Dotty. Her husband, thin and nervous-looking, joined her. In a clear, well-modulated voice she said, "You strike me as a sensible fellow. Can't you resolve this problem?"

"Don't listen to her!" the plump blonde woman screamed, pushing Dotty out of her path and placing herself between Bert and the matron.

"Who are you shoving, you kook?" Dotty asked, as she shoved the fat blonde back, knocking her bifocals to the floor.

"Oh, my God, it's a race riot," gasped the matron, grabbing her husband and heading for the door.

The big blonde squatted on the floor. "Goddamn shits," she muttered, her arms moving in ever widening circles as she searched for her glasses.

"Come on, let's get out of here before I really get mad," declared Dotty, who had hold of Bert's suit jacket and was pulling him towards the door.

"Man, do you believe these people?" she asked as they got on the elevator.

"Who was the big broad?"

"Judy, one of these spoiled Jewish brats, still fightin' her parents. Spent her whole life in college. She's behind the rent strike. Her parents pay her rent. If she'd lived in Harlem and had tried to pull that crap, she'd have her ass handed to her so fast, make her head spin.''

"I'm not getting into that dog fight," Bert declared. The elevator stopped at their floor.

"That's what you think," Dotty responded as they crossed the outside hallway. "They ain't gonna fire Caesar because he's Black. They're gonna get *you* to do it. You watch."

"By the way," Bert said as they entered the apartment, "Henry reminds me of somebody, a person I've seen somewhere."

"You're kidding," exclaimed Dotty, taking off her sweater.

"No. He reminds me of somebody."

"You didn't watch much TV as a kid, did you?"

"Why?"

"He looks like Howdy Doody, Bert."

"Oh yeah, that's who." They both broke out laughing.

Bert was in early the next morning. The business plans were flowing in from all over the world. He and Bridget were prepared to work overtime until the presentation day at the end of the month.

"Let's see," he said. "I need to talk to Taylor in London. Are they six hours behind or ahead of us?"

"Ahead," Bridget responded. "I'll try him."

A few minutes later, she buzzed. "He's not back from lunch yet. He'll get back to you. I'm going down to the mail room to collect more plans."

"Would you shut the door as you go, please? I got to finish reading these."

Several hours later, Bert looked up, annoyed at a sharp knock and the door opening. His glare softened. "Come in," he muttered to the shoe shine man, who had already

48

invaded the room. "But I don't have time to talk today," Bert warned, continuing to leaf through a book.

The little man left his kit beside Bert and walked over to the painting of the Benin king. "Three million bucks," he mused, half to himself, and looked at it from several angles.

The tall executive continued to read.

Big Bucks sauntered over to Bert's desk and squatted in front of him; the bolt on the box gave off a sharp report.

Spotting the caption on the book Bert was reading, the old man murmured, "Five year business plan. Y'all in big business kill me, all these five year plans. Don't mean a damn thing." He started polishing the shoes.

"Well, if you understood them, you'd know why all the progressive companies use them," the younger man muttered, not looking up.

Big Bucks gave up any pretense of shining shoes. A wide grin settled on his face. "Now you a smart man, got you an MBA and all that—tell me how you gonna plan for five years from now when maybe ain't none of us still be around."

Bert knew he should get on with his work, but the temptation was too great. He said, "A five year plan gives you a general direction. It doesn't give you any exact answers."

"Trouble is, it can give you wrong answers. That's what I told the Chairman."

Bert glanced at him. "Oh, bullshit," the executive snorted, turning a page in the book.

"Chairman didn't think so."

The thick book slipped from Bert's fingers as his eyes rose to meet Big Bucks'. "You're kidding. He's the one who brought business planning into this company, and I'm sure it's gonna take more than you to get him to drop it." He picked up another plan and began leafing through it.

The old man went down on one knee. "It's them five year plans what's killin' industry," he declared as he labored over the shoes.

"Looking for profits every quarter is the problem, not long term planning," the younger man said with a smug smile, and closed the book.

"Five year plan tell you that oil was goin' through the roof?" the gnome asked, sitting back on his haunches.

"That was unique—you know, different."

"I know what unique means, I read like you do—guess the depression in Detroit was unique. Ford and them got five year plans?"

The taller man gritted his teeth in silence.

"What the problem is," Hiawatha continued, beginning to pace in front of Bert's chair, as if he were lecturing, "boys at the top been payin' too much attention to them five year plans, instead of gettin' they ass out in the field. That's what happened at Chrysler."

"You seem to have all the answers," Bert snapped. "I guess if you had been President, they wouldn't have gone bankrupt?"

"That's right."

"And just how would you have performed that miracle?"

"Jes as soon as I begin to see any red ink on them reports, I wouldn't hold no meetin', I get right out there on the spot, and if the manager can't give me no good answers, well, he's gone. That's what Eyeococo did, when he got in."

The telephone interrupted them.

"London calling," the operator announced, "for Mrs. Mattox."

"She's my secretary, operator. I'm expecting the call. Go ahead."

"I'm sorry, sir. My party will speak only to Mrs. Mat-. tox."

"Are you sure it's not for Mr. Davis?"

"Quite sure, sir."

"Well, she's not here right now."

"My party will call back later. Thank you." The phone went dead.

"I wonder what that's all about?" Bert wondered out loud.

"Probably got some action goin' in London, " the old man said with a little grin.

"Oh, come on," Bert said. "I doubt she's been out of the States."

"Huh? With them two gifts she got, the world will come to her," Daddy replied, picking up his kit and leaving.

Bridget returned, her arms full of books.

"There was a phone call for you, from London."

He watched her face turn crimson as she dropped the books on his desk.

The phone rang. "It's probably London. May I take it in here?"

"Sure," Bert said with a grin. He closed the door behind him and made his way down to the cafeteria.

Harry, his bright blue tie clashing with his brown suit, was sitting by himself in the dingy, half empty room. Bert plunked his dried-out hamburger and coffee on the Formica. Harry's empty plate was in front of him, and he was sipping his coffee.

"Well, well, it's Big Bucks' buddy. I understand you two are getting along real well."

"Well enough," Bert said, shoving his empty tray over to a table loaded with empty dishes. He bit into the burger and grimaced. "You should see his chicks."

"Where'd you see this?"

"I had a drink with him—you should have seen this one called Sugar." Harry's eyes lit up as Bert described her.

Just then, Jim walked in, as the cafeteria began to fill up.

"Greetings," he said, lowering his food to the table.

"Bert here's been telling me about Hiawatha's women," Harry volunteered.

"Oh?" remarked Jim, wiping his spoon off with a napkin.

"Not only that, but he's introduced Bucks to the world of art." Then, to Bert, he said, "He seems quite taken with your painting. Can't get over that something like that could cost so much. He thinks you're gonna help him get in on the action."

"Shit, I never told him I was an expert. I told him it was my wife's hobby."

"Well, as far as he's concerned, you're the expert who's going to help him make a lot of money."

"He'll wait a long time."

"I wouldn't be too hasty. Summer's coming, and he might invite you out on his boat," Jim said.

Harry drained his coffee cup and said, "You'll have to excuse me, I gotta go, but I'm sure Jim will fill you in."

"What kind of boat?"

"A big baby. Understand it sleeps fourteen—and he has some wild parties on board," Jim concluded with a twinkle.

"When does he take it out, if he works all the time?"

"On Sundays, after church."

"That scamp religious?"

"Claims he never misses. Teaches Sunday School."

"Boy, I'd love to be a fly on the wall while he's teaching," Bert said, breaking into a short laugh. "How does he justify all his womanizing?"

"Claims he gets authority from the Old Testament—brought in the Bible one day and showed me chapter and verse."

"Did it?" asked Bert in amazement.

"Didn't to me, but he's totally convinced. Ask him to bring it in, see for yourself."

"I might," Bert said, draining his cup, and added as he got up to go, "I'll tell you what I learn." Jim began reading the newspaper. Bert threaded his way out of the dining room.

CHAPTER SEVEN

Bert knew that something was up. It was the middle of the week and Bridget was wearing a sheer, low cut blue blouse. His office carried the scent of her perfume.

"Here we are," she sang out, and placed the coffee on his desk, surrounded by cookies she had baked.

"Okay, okay," Bert said, "let's have it."

"What?" she asked, eyes wide open.

"Come on," her boss said, "I know when I'm being buttered up." His secretary had remained an enigma to him since he had met her two years before. She had come directly from California, where she had worked on a feminist newspaper. During the employment interview, he'd asked, quite innocently, if she was married. With a little smile, she had responded, "It's against the law to ask that. Besides," she had concluded softly, "it's really not your concern."

"To tell the truth," Bridget whispered, "there is a little something I'd like to discuss with you."

"You're sure you want to tell me about it? You could go to Personnel."

"No, no, I want to talk to you. Mind if I close the door?" Her movement stirred the scent of her perfume. "I have to take off for two weeks."

"Now? During business plan time? That's crazy—you know we're up to our asses in alligators."

"I know," she said in a wistful voice, "but something critical has come up, and I have to have the time."

Bert silently wondered who had died.

Looking up at her boss, a sheepish smile playing on her face, she said, "Anton wants me to meet his family."

Bert gawked.

"Anton Paschall's my friend in London. He wants me to visit him—to decide if we're really meant for each other."

An embarrassed grin broke out on Bert's face. "You don't have to tell me all this, you know."

"Oh, I want to," she said. "I can't confide in anybody else. After all, I can't very well tell my husband," she ended in almost a whisper.

"I guess not," Bert replied, still staring at her.

"I got to confide in somebody."

"What are you going to tell Leo?"

"I don't know—we have an open marriage, but I don't know if it's that open."

"That's pretty damn open," Bert declared.

"But Anton's so wonderful," she burbled. "I really must go. I'd never forgive myself if I didn't.

"I guess you know what you're doing," Bert said with a sigh. "Better get a temporary and teach her as much as you can before you go."

"I really hate to leave you in the lurch like this."

"What happens if Leo finds out?"

"We'll cross that little bridge when we come to it,"
she said, giving him a little conspiratorial smile.

"Boy, I'll tell you, she's really got balls," Bert said
that night as he held a painting up for Dotty.

"To the left a little...down on the right. Hold it right
there—I want to see it from the door."

"Hurry, will you? The damn thing's heavy."

"Look, I beat out fifteen other people for this Bearden.
Least you could do is hold it straight."

"Looks like a broad taking a bath to me," Bert muttered, eyeing the canvas with its vivid blues and blacks,
its few touches of grey: one woman standing in an old-
fashioned tub, washing herself, being watched over by a
second, old, black-faced with yellow eyes.

"Just a little to the right—hold it."

"Thank God," Bert said as he marked the place.

"You realize what this is gonna be worth in a few
years? I'll be able to quit nursing."

"By the way, Big Bucks saw the Benin King and wants
to get into art."

"When did that jive turkey discover art?"

"When I told him what the original cost."

"Figures," Dotty said, tapping a nail into the wall.
She stepped back and looked admiringly at the painting.
"What was that about Bridget?"

"She's going to London to meet her lover."

"Really? Who?"

"Don't know. I just know his name is Anton Paschall
and he's a lawyer, or barrister, as they call them over there."

"Must have something to take her way over there,"
she said with a little grin. "Good for her!"

"Good?"

"Yeah, I never did think too much of Leo. Eyes too shifty for me. I'd never trust him."

"She's married to him—what's his eyes got to do with it?"

"I don't know why she told you all her business."

"Hell, she's taking off two weeks in the busiest time of the year."

There was a sharp rap at the door.

"I forgot to tell you," Dotty said. "Henry's been looking for you—there's an emergency meeting tonight. They're waitin' for you to fire Caesar."

The tall redhead entered. "Hi, Dotty. Hi, Bert. Big doings tonight. We need our key man."

Dotty rolled her eyes and excused herself.

"Bert, we need you," Henry said, then, dropping his voice, continued, "he's at it again."

"Who this time?" Bert stole a quick look at Henry. Sure enough, he was a dead ringer for Howdy Doody. Bert fought unsuccessfully the smile that came to his face.

"Mrs. Bash, on eleven."

He's got good taste, Bert thought. "Henry," he said, with a serious look, "we've got to act."

"My very thought," Henry replied, moving towards the door. "Come on. The committee's waiting downstairs."

The yellow-walled room was filled with smoke. Sitting around the long portable table that exhibited patches of red, yellow, and black paint were the six men who, with Bert and Henry, made up the co-op Executive Council. The smoke from a cigar in the ashtray curled up towards the ceiling. Three of them held cups of coffee.

Sol, a bald-headed man in a grey uniform, his name stitched in red on his shirt pocket, had just finished ticking off on his fingers the reasons why the Council should fire Caesar. He paused and cleared his throat as the last two men sat down. "On the other hand," he continued, "to be perfectly fair, who among us is without sin?" and proceeded to refute his previous points.

"I don't believe this," Bert muttered to Henry.

"Come on, Sol," someone said. "Finish already."

A short, stocky man, almost bald, dressed in corduroy pants and hiking boots, shouted, "Let's hear from Bert."

Unwinding his long frame, Bert looked over the group and said in a loud voice, "Let's vote on firing him, now."

Seven pairs of eyes looked up at him in stunned silence.

"Where is it written," demanded Sol, "we should fire a poor man with a family for a few transgressions?"

"Transgressions my ass!" Bert exploded. "He's been grabbing behinds all over the building."

"Maybe he's a mental case," someone suggested.

"Bullcrap," Bert declared. "Let's vote."

"Yes, yes," responded Henry, his button eyes bright, and a wide smile spread across his freckled face.

Five hands rose to signify that Caesar must go.

After the meeting, the members of the Council gathered around Bert and congratulated him on his forthright action.

Sol caught up with Bert as he reached the elevator. "If we've made a mistake, let it be on your head."

"So be it," Bert snapped as the doors closed.

"That didn't take long," Dotty said, looking up from the TV set. "Want coffee?"

"Yeah, thanks," her husband sighed.

"What happened?" she asked from the kitchen.

"We fired Caesar."

"How?"

"Huh?" he asked, engrossed in the late news.

"How? How?" Dotty asked, nudging him and almost spilling the coffee.

"I finally convinced them," Bert muttered.

"What'd I tell you?" she exclaimed as she put down the coffee and snuggled into his lap. "I knew they'd get you to do it."

A few days before she left for London, Bridget introduced her replacement, Linda Chen.

"I think she'll do very well," Bridget told Bert. "She's a hard worker and I've told her that this is a very, very important function."

The business plan presentations went smoothly, but, while generally pleased with Linda, Bert noticed that the incoming phone calls had trickled down to almost nothing, and asked Linda about it.

"You are a very important man," she declared. "You get all important calls."

The next day, Bert noticed that six calls had come in before Linda buzzed.

"It's Mr. Wilson. He say he must talk to you."

"Put him on." He could hear her resigned sigh.

"What's with your secretary? I've been trying for days to get through to you," Harry said.

"What are you talking about? Nobody told me you called."

"Hell, your secretary grilled me for ten minutes yesterday. I finally gave up."

"God!" Bert muttered. "I hope the Chairman didn't call."

"I hope not, for your sake—what I wanted to tell you was that Big Bucks was in this morning. He still wants to get into art in the worst way—seems that someone told him it's a hedge against inflation. I told him that if he invited you and Dotty out on his boat, you might be more cooperative."

"Well, we might at that."

"You owe me one," Harry said and hung up.

Bert buzzed Linda. "Sit down, please," the executive said as she entered the office. She was small and frail, weighed hardly a hundred pounds, and wore her black hair in a page boy. Her eyes, slanted by her high cheekbones, were as black as coal; her head darted back and forth like a bird's. When she typed, her hands flew over the keys. She sat on the front of her chair as if she would fly off at the slightest sound.

"Am I doing everything correctly, Mr. Davis?" There was a pleading quality in her eyes. "Please tell me if I'm not pleasing you."

"You are. Oh yes," Bert assured her. "It's just that—"

"Yes?" She moved to the tip of her chair.

"It's that—well, you can't question all the people who call—know what I mean?"

"I don't please you," she said, beginning to cry.

"Yes you do!" Bert declared, pushing the box of Kleenex over to her.

"Bridget told me no one was to waste your time," she sniffled. "Mr. Wilson is not a serious man."

"Look, Linda, I'm happy with the way you've taken hold of this job," Bert lied with all the conviction he could muster.

With a proud smile, crumpled Kleenex in hand, Linda rose from her seat, paused at the door. "I'll close this. Important man cannot be disturbed."

The executive shrugged his shoulders helplessly.

Bert had just finished his mail when he heard a ruckus outside his office.

"No! No! You must not go in there."

"Girl, that's my customer in there."

"I don't care if he's your customer, he's an important man."

"I ain't disturbin' him. I come to shine his shoes," Bert heard the old man say as he opened the door.

"This man will disturb you," exclaimed Linda, throwing her frail body between them.

Pushing the secretary aside, Big Bucks strode past Bert into the office.

Linda's face clouded.

"It's okay," Bert declared. "He's important. I'll explain later."

Mollified, Linda said in a very serious tone, "We talk later," and marched to her desk.

"Goddamn," Bucks declared, "she's worse than the CIA. She look like one of them boat people to me—when your girl comin' back?"

"She's Chinese, not Korean—damnit," Bert groused, leafing through a stack of reports, "can't find a thing."

"Don't know how to treat womens," Hiawatha declared as he spread out his brush and rags.

"She's just irresponsible, taking off like that in the busiest time of the year."

"Careful now. She got her good points," the old man replied, putting on a coat of polish.

"I know," Bert said, "she got big boobs."

"That ain't what I mean," Big Bucks said indignantly, then in a wistful voice continued, "though Lord knows she sure got a proud pair."

"Then you tell me why she'd take off like that?"

The old man laid down his brush, sighed, and said, "For an educated man you don't know very much, does you?"

"I'm all ears," Bert snapped.

Linda brought in the mail, stood and eyed them suspiciously, then walked out.

"Trouble with her is, she probably ain't had her field ploughed in some time," the old man observed as he watched Linda disappear through the door.

"That's your answer to everything, isn't it?"

"Yeah? Well you young cats don't know nothin' about treatin' womens. Now, first thing you got to realize is that age make a big difference in womens—"

"I heard you don't keep a woman once she's over twenty-five."

"That's a fact," the old man said as he stood over the executive.

"Why?"

"Stop interuppin' and I'll tell you. Now, womens have gone through a lot of changes in recent times. Men cain't keep 'em down the way they used to."

"I know all that," Bert interjected.

"You gonna let me tell this? Well—older womens been told all they lives that they can't do nothin'. Now with things openin' up, they's confused. Younger womens know they can do most things, so they goes for it."

"Bridget's about twenty-five. She sure seems confused to me, taking off and leaving her husband."

"She ain't confused," the gnome grinned. "She know what she doin'. She gonna do alright for herself. We talks a lot about real estate. It what she take in night school."

"Bridget in real estate? You've got to be kidding. What's she planing to be, a sales agent? Hell, she got a better job right here."

"That all you think there is in real estate?" Bucks asked, leisurely stroking the shoe with his brush.

"What else?"

"Now that's a real profession, and that girl's goin' 'bout it the right way." There was more than a hint of indignation in Big Bucks' voice.

"You go to real estate school too?" the tall executive teased.

"School of hard knocks," he snorted, going back to the shoes. "Bought me some ole houses when city was almost givin' 'em away. Fixed 'em up, sold 'em for a pretty penny—'course, took me fifteen years."

Big Bucks smiled, brushed Bert's shoes, and then asked, "You and the wife like to fish?" Putting down the brush, he continued, "I'm takin' the boat out for a little spin on Sunday with some of my business pals."

"Business pals?"

"Peoples I work with."

"We'd be delighted. What time?"

"Right after Sunday School, about twelve." Hiawatha got up and stretched his legs.

"Don't tell me you're a churchman," Bert asked, feigning ignorance.

The gnome pivoted and stared. "Man, I been a deacon for ten years—what you talkin' 'bout?"

"Gee, Bucks, Sugar and Cindy don't seem to be the kind of company a churchman should be keeping."

"Church peoples some of the biggest sinners, always tryin' to sneak around. Mine's all out front. Besides, it tell you right in the Bible, it's all right to have plenty womens, long as it's only one at a time."

"Where?"

"You recall where it say you ain't supposed to let no seed spill on the ground?"

"Yeah, but that just means you're not supposed to masturbate."

"That's why you got to have lots of womens. When one leave, you gets another." A self-satisfied smile covered Daddy's face as he went back to the shoes.

"By the way, where do we meet you?"

"City Island. Windom Boatyard."

It was almost noon the next day when Bridget walked in—disheveled, a bruise over her right eye, no make-up, red veins overshadowing the blue of her eyes.

"Sorry I'm late," she snapped. "It's that damn subway."

Bert said nothing and continued to work.

"Jet lag?" Bert inquired innocently when she brought his coffee later.

"Leo," she responded.

"What happened?"

"I guess the marriage wasn't as open as I thought." She gingerly touched her bruise, and a wry smile came over her face.

"How was London?"

"Very nice, well worth the trip. Oh, Mr. Davis, he took me out to his home in the country. It was just like a travel poster. His family was lovely, and in London we ate in the best of places."

"You think you were meant for each other?" Bert asked, sipping his coffee and looking up at her.

"I'm not really sure. Both he and Leo have their strong points."

"Looks like you've got a big decision to make."

"Not really." Her old smile returned. "I plan to keep them both."

CHAPTER EIGHT

Bert and Dotty entered the crowded elevator together
that Sunday morning.

"Do I look okay?" Dotty whispered.

"Fine," Bert replied out of the corner of his mouth,
looking at her tight designer jeans that matched his. "You
just have to wear shoes that won't slip."

The doors opened to the ground floor; there staring at
them was the big, blonde woman, her body bulging out of
her Kent State warmup suit. She sat like a giant owl behind a folding card table, blinking behind her bifocals. A
sheet of paper taped to the edge of her table read *Save the
Super.* Spotting the couple, she looked away, asking others
to sign her petition. Several people stopped to talk.

"Well, so much for firing Caesar," Dotty said.

"My God," Bert exclaimed, "that's all we need," as
they passed a second, much larger, table further down the
hall, where tenants were being asked not to pay rent until
pets were allowed. A large yellow sign on the wall read *No
Pets—No Pay.*

"Weirdos are really out this morning," Dotty commented, following Bert out the big glass doors.

"About time for us to move to the suburbs—second one this week," Bert said as he retrieved a ticket from the wiper of his metallic grey BMW.

"It ain't that bad. Besides, suburbs don't want Black folks. Oh—I forgot my sunglasses."

"Get in the car," Bert commanded. "We're late. We can buy a pair out there."

He turned at the sign for City Island.

"You know where you're going?"

"I'm following his directions. Damn place looks like a fishing village, and right here in the Bronx," Bert said as they passed store after store that offered bait and fishing tackle.

"I think that's the road you want. I used to come out here with my grandfather, long time ago."

They passed a number of seafood restaurants and suddenly came up on the Windom Boatyard. The clubhouse was a modern glass and wood structure built on the end of a short dock, at the edge of the boat basin. Boats of every size were moored in the basin, rocking in the wake of others making for the bay. It was a glorious day; two seagulls wheeled overhead, calling to each other.

"Is that it?" Dotty asked, shielding her eyes from the sun.

"Looks like it," Bert replied, maneuvering into a parking space.

Outside the clubhouse stood Malik, dressed in a white shirt that came almost to his knees, over black pants. A white skull cap on his head, he moved toward the couple.

"Wait till you meet this one," Bert muttered to his wife.

"Dotty, this is Malik."

"Salam Alekum," Dotty greeted.

"Alukum ah salam," Malik responded, showing a smile for the first time. "Sister," he said, looking at Bert, "I had no idea."

Malik grasped Bert in a warm handshake. His face seemed to have a glow. "Brother, I've misjudged you—come on in—they're waiting."

The club was carpeted throughout in green, a large anchor woven into it. On a leather sofa looking out over the basin sat Big Bucks, flanked by two men.

"They're here," announced Malik softly. The three men rose to greet them. Hiawatha, in addition to his white pants and shoes, sported a blue blazer with a gold-crusted emblem on the breast pocket. His captain's hat sat at a jaunty angle.

"Welcome, welcome," he said. "This here is Winston McIntosh and Hector Nunez."

"My wife, Dotty," Bert announced.

Winston McIntosh stood over six feet. His honey brown hair flecked with grey and his large flat nose gave him the air of an ex-boxer. He wore a craggy smile and looked every inch the athlete in his striped tank top and shorts. His grip was firm.

"I'm with Manny Hanny. Mr. Jackson tells me you're with American Instruments."

"Yes, I am," Bert replied.

The couple waited for Nunez, a short, chubby man, whose thick black moustache contrasted with his olive skin, to introduce himself. Instead, he stood up in his grease-stained palm beach suit, complete with tie, blinking at them, chewing on his huge moustache.

"Hector's my accountant," Big Bucks explained. "He don't say too much."

Hector continued to blink and stare.

"Les go," the gnome announced, leading the way. He paused as they walked down the slight incline. "Say," he said to Dotty, "understand you from Harlem. What part?"

"One-thirty-first and Seventh. We had a funeral home—"

"You ain't Sam Downey's girl, is you?"

"Yes," Dotty said, beginning to bristle.

"Hell, I used to play poker with Sam—you ain't the youngest one, who was so wild?"

Dotty's mouth clamped shut, the muscles in her jaws distended.

"She's the art expert," Bert interjected quickly.

"No shit. And you've grown up to be a fine girl. You take art in college?"

"She's a nurse," Bert responded, not wanting to risk an answer from Dotty. "She does art as a hobby."

"Well, that's *nice*. Come on, Cindy's waitin'," Bucks said as he moved to catch up with the others.

"What's Manny Hanny?" Dotty asked her husband.

"Manufacturers Hanover Bank. Had you seen him before?"

"No, I left before my father's poker playing days began."

"I wonder what he's into," Bert mused as they walked after the old man. "You got to have at least a high-six-figure account to rate that type of service."

"You mean that guy's his own private banker?"

"He ain't out here for his health."

"Wonder how he feels out here with a bunch of Blacks on Sunday instead of being home with his family."

"That's how he keeps his job."

Hiawatha Jackson and his companions stopped in front of a gleaming white cruiser that took up half the dock. A solid blue stripe bar ran below the deck. Several pennants flew from the mast. On the keel, in large gold letters ran the legend, *BIG BUCKS City Island.*

"That's the name of it, Big Bucks?"

"What else—damn, it's big," Bert said as they joined the little group going aboard.

"Come aboard, mates," Cindy called down from the flying bridge. She saluted with her right hand and held a drink with the other.

"She's fifty-three feet," Big Bucks boasted, looking up at the ship as Winston and Hector climbed the little ladder to the deck. "Couldn't be nothin' but a mess mate in the Navy, but I promised myself oncet I got out, I was gonna own one of these mothers."

Cindy reached the deck the same time they did.

"You remember Bert, dontcha? This here's his wife."

"Hi, Bert," she purred in a low sultry voice, giving Dotty a faint nod. Cindy looked as if she had been poured into her white jeans, and her light green blouse gave way to flawlessly smooth brown arms. She wore a long gold chain and large matching earrings. "Cocktail for you," she breathed to the old man, putting a glass in his hand. Hiawatha grinned and accepted it.

"Who the hell is Cindy?" muttered Dotty as the couple moved off.

"Bucks' girl."

"She better stay that way, or both of you'll get a new set of teeth—old buzzard ought to be ashamed of himself, runnin' around with someone young enough to be his granddaughter."

"Oh, come on Dotty. Let's see the rest of the boat."

"You've got to see below deck," said Winston, coming up behind them and leading them down the reddish-orange carpeted ladder. "That's the galley," he said, indicating the gleaming stainless steel cabinets and the large refrigerator across from the dining booth. "And there," he said, pointing to a cabin down a few more steps, "is the crew's sleeping quarters."

"It's bigger than our apartment," Dotty exclaimed.

"Bigger than most," Winston affirmed. "Look at this." He pulled open a teak-paneled door, revealing a washer and dryer.

"Oh, my God!" she exclaimed. "I don't believe it."

Smiling broadly and enjoying himself, Winston said, "You ain't seen nothin' yet." He led them through a narrow passage to the rear of the boat, paused, and slid open a panel in the wall. There lay a 500-horsepower engine, looking as if it belonged on a giant earth mover. Winston held up two fingers. "One on each side." The door at the end of the passage opened to a stateroom. In the center was a huge round bed.

"This," Winston announced, "is the captain's cabin." Bert caught his reflection in the mirrored ceiling.

"He calls it his pleasure palace," Winston said apologetically.

When the trio reached the main deck, Cindy was stretched out on the full length paisley-patterned couch. Across from her, Big Bucks sat in a matching swivel chair.

"Bert," the old man exclaimed, "I'm gonna show you what we skippers got to know," indicating the bridge, across from where they sat. "See this?" he asked, grasping a large metal wheel almost his size. He gave it a few turns for emphasis. "This how I controls it. Now then, that's my radar, good for forty-eight miles."

Bert whistled appreciatively.

"Malik," the skipper commanded, "turn on some air conditioning. It's hot in here."

Cindy reached over and turned on the hi-fi.

"Piped all over the ship," Bucks boasted.

Cindy rose, slipped her arm through Bucks, and began to sway with the music. He suddenly took Dotty's arm. "Now we gonna have a little talk about art," he said, propelling the two women towards the deck.

Cindy pouted, a frown taking over her lovely face.

"Don't be gettin' no attitude. 'Bout time you learned somethin' 'bout our art," he boomed as they walked out on deck.

Malik smiled to himself as he fiddled with the controls.

"What a sight, huh?" Bert asked when he and Winston went out on the aft deck.

"Great day," the other responded. "What is it you do at American Instruments?"

"Director of Planning. You know, business planning, economic forecasting, that kind of thing." Bert looked across the channel at a wooded island.

"That's a big job. Where did you come from?"

Bert smiled to himself. It never failed: Whites always wanted to know how you got there.

"Got my MBA at NYU, and started out at IBM."

Winston let out a low whistle. "Some background—I was at NYU myself. That was quite a few years ago."

Feeling he had divulged enough, Bert asked, "What's your connection with Bucks?"

"Oh, Mr. Jackson? Why, he's one of the bank's important clients," Winston explained as he walked over to the bar, reached up, took two glasses from the rack on the ceiling, and asked, "Martini?"

"Come on," Bert snorted, accepting his glass. "A shoe shine man?"

"How well do you know him?" the other man asked, his grey eyes focused on Bert.

"Just around the company. The soap and freshener business couldn't be that good."

Winston sat back in a bamboo chair, smiled, and said, "You don't get an account executive unless your account is seven figures."

Bert gasped. "How could he have that kind of money?"

"Real estate," Winston replied with a wide smile, enjoying Bert's shock.

"Real estate?"

"Come on, y'all, les go, time for service!" Big Bucks suddenly exclaimed, sweeping into the room with Dotty still on his arm. She wore a scowl and rolled her eyes at Bert. Cindy trailed them, wearing a smile.

Bert looked quizzically at Winston, who motioned to the upper deck with his head.

The view from there was extraordinary. The whole harbor opened up to the sea—white clouds overhead, the wheeling, squawking seagulls fighting over a hot dog dropped from a passing boat by a six-year-old boy, who watched them in fascination.

Cindy took Winston's and Hector's hands. Hiawatha grasped Bert's and Dotty's to form a circle. Malik stood at the bridge that was a reproduction of the one below, aloof from the group, and checked the gauges.

The old man bent his head. Cindy, in a clear, sweet voice, sang the first verse of *Amazing Grace,* so loudly that a man swabbing the deck of his boat looked up. Everyone but Hector mumbled the words; he hummed.

As the handclasps slipped, Malik threw a switch, and the vibrations of the motors could be felt throughout the boat.

"Like to have a little word with my maker 'fore I go to sea," the old man said by way of explanation.

As the boat slid away from the dock, Hector, chewing on his moustache, poured from a large pitcher of mixed martinis and filled every glass, ignoring several protests, a fiendish smile fixed on his face.

"I'm gonna help Malik take this mother out to sea," Bucks said, trying to wrest the wheel from him.

"Careful, my brother," Malik protested softly as the boat eased into the channel.

There was a loud blast on a horn somewhere in front of them, followed by a string of curses that came closer as a small boat came along side.

"You stupid sonofabitch," screamed the man in it— "if you don't know what you're doing, stay in Harlem or wherever you come from!" His wife glared up at the little group clustered at the rail. "I ought to report you to the Coast Guard," the angry man continued. "My wife and I could be dead now."

"He could," Malik murmured. "He had the right of way."

"I don't like his attitude," Dotty snapped, her jaws bulging. "I'll handle him."

"No, no," said the old man. "I'll handle this." With unbelievable agility he jumped down to the smaller boat. He huddled with the couple in a low confidential tone. Bert saw him reach in his pocket. A few minutes later, he called up. "Give me a hand." Two arms, one White, the other Brown, reached over and pulled him aboard. The couple, now smiling gaily, waved goodbye to Mr. Jackson. The man revved his motor and put out to sea.

"Sure seemed to make them happy," Cindy commented, watching the boat make its way into the bay.

"Well," grinned Jackson, "when you has a little misunderstanding, why, you jes spreads a little sunshine."

The ship vibrated again, and Malik, unimpeded, guided them out into the channel. No one spoke as the boat got underway, awed by the silence of the water. "That's Stepping Stones, and we'll soon be under the Throgs Neck Bridge," the Muslim said softly.

Cindy snuggled up against the old man; he grinned and, without excusing themselves, they went below.

Dotty curled up with a book and Bert joined Winston, who was sipping his drink and watching a line of rusty garbage barges being pulled by red and black tugboats.

"Phew," Bert exclaimed as a breeze brought them the barge smells.

"That's Riker's Island." Winston pointed to the small body of land covered by tall buildings with barred windows.

"He's a quiet one," Bert murmured, indicating with his head the chubby man in a suit and tie who was moving toward them, hanging onto the rail. Just as Hector reached them, the boat began to pitch and shudder. Hector's eyes got as big as saucers.

"What in the hell?" Bert exploded as he hung on to the rail.

"Hellgate," explained Winston, "always rough." Then he let fly a torrent of Spanish.

A faint smile of understanding appeared on the short man's face, his eyes blinking rapidly behind his big round glasses.

"No hables Espanol?" Hector asked, looking at Bert.

"Que pasa?" was all that would come to Bert's mind.

"Muy bueno," Hector responded, smiling and blinking behind his tortoise-shell round glasses. The only Spanish Bert could think of was the warning sign on the subway that read *El tren el subterreno es muy peligroso.* Bert pointed at the water, which had become calmer, and said, ''Es is muy peligroso.''

''Yes, sea bery dangerous,'' Hector said solemnly, and went inside to lie down.

''How the hell can he be an accountant if he can't speak any better English than that?''

''He's one of the best—there's the South Street Seaport over there.''

''If he's so good, why isn't he with one of the big eight?''

''He's good enough to be, believe me—he's sort of strange. Can you imagine his working for one of the top accounting firms with that get-up?''

''No, but couldn't someone just tell him to dress better? Hell, all he has to do is wear a pin-striped suit and black wingtip shoes and long black socks. He sure could do something about his English.''

''Hector's convinced that the country will eventually become bilingual,'' Winston said with a grin. ''He doesn't want to waste time perfecting his English.''

''Doesn't it bother his accounting?''

''Oh, he reads excellently. In fact, he helped Mr. Jackson make it big in real estate.

''Really?''

''Yup. Seems that Hector couldn't get a job so he opened his own practice. Mr. Jackson went to him, I guess because his price was right.'' Winston gave a little blush, looked at his glass. ''Bankers shouldn't talk while they drink.''

As they walked in the main cabin, squeals from below deck became louder and ended in one loud shriek, followed by silence.

Malik, at the bridge, shook his head, a disgusted look on his face.

"Dirty old man," Dotty commented, looking up from her book.

"There she is," Winston exclaimed as the Statue of Liberty came into view. He and Bert went to the upper deck for a better view. A Staten Island ferry passed going in the opposite direction. "There are the Narrows," the banker said. "We're out to sea."

"What are you, the company historian?" Bert asked.

"No, I was just around Mr. Jackson from the start. About twenty years ago—I was just a young loan officer at the time—I made a loan to him. Well, you can imagine management reaction in those days when I made a loan to a Black man, or Colored as they were called. If it hadn't been secured by good property, I suspect I'd have been fired on the spot. Coming from Maine, I didn't know any better. Anyway, a few years later, Hector discovered a tax loophole and advised Mr. Jackson to buy up as many old houses in Harlem and Bedford Stuyvesant as he could, and take advantage of the rapid depreciation clause he had discovered. In no time, Mr. Jackson's real estate firm was worth several million."

Bert stared at Winston in disbelief.

"About that time," the banker continued, "civil rights was in full swing, and as you can imagine, I was a big hero with the same guys who were trying to fire me a few years before."

"But...why does he still shine shoes?"

"Claims it keeps him in touch with the real people," Winston said with a grin.

"Here y'all is," Hiawatha said, following Cindy up the stairs.

"I need another drink after all that action," Cindy said, going out to the bar on the aft deck.

"We gonna want to talk some more about art," the old man said.

"No we don't," Dotty snapped, and opened her book. Bucks went out to join Cindy.

"What happened?" Bert asked.

"Wanted me to consult for free," Dotty snorted indignantly, putting her book aside. "The little bastard had the nerve to tell me that working with the art should be my reward. I told him a few things."

"I'll bet you did," Bert said with a grin.

Malik, seeing the couple alone, walked over. "Brother and Sister," he greeted them. "Thank you for trying to teach brother Jackson about our heritage."

Bert looked at the unmanned wheel in horror.

Malik, following his eyes, broke into a shy smile and explained, "It's on automatic pilot."

"Dotty's the one who knows about art," Bert said, much relieved.

"All he's interested in is money," Dotty responded firmly.

"The appreciation will come," Malik said softly. "Give him time. He's still being driven by excesses of the flesh."

"How long you been in the Faith?" Dotty asked.

"Three years now. I dropped out of Hampton in my senior year."

"What are you doing acting like a chauffeur to him, with your education?" Bert demanded.

"My mission is to serve," murmurered the earnest young man. "If I can get my brother to correct some of his ways, he could be a mighty force for Black people."

"From what I understand, he's doing quite well the way he is," Bert commented.

"It's going to take some—"

"Les go, Malik," Big Bucks hollered as he arrived on the main deck. "We goin' in now."

CHAPTER NINE

The floor was in an uproar when Bert arrived late from a breakfast meeting with the Governing Board of the co-op.

"What the hell is going on?" he asked, walking into his secretary's cubicle, away from the din in the hall.

"Oh, Mr. Davis, you haven't heard," Bridget said, looking up from the newspaper. "The English company, Stokingham, is trying to take us over."

"*What?*" he exclaimed, taking the paper she thrust at him. "...It says here that they have almost five percent of the stock."

"Can they do it?" Bridget asked, her eyes as big as saucers, following him into his office.

"Naw," scoffed Bert. "Can you believe this? 'He says the stockholders would be better served if he took over and cleaned house.' Hell, he's a raider, not a businessman."

"But can he do it?" she insisted.

"Stokingham is just an English hustler. This is a big corporation. He's going to get one hell of a shock if he thinks he's gonna take us on."

She picked up the phone on its first ring. "It's the Chairman's office. He wants to meet with all executives in ten minutes."

Bert joined the others who strode down the green carpeted hallway with its dark wood paneling and sparse light, making it look like a mausoleum, and filed into the admiral's large oak-paneled office. Along one wall, on a narrow table, stood models of American battleships. On the wall over his massive desk hung a ceremonial sword and a torn Japanese flag, a source of embarrassment to anyone bringing in Japanese customers.

Bert sunk into a deep cushioned seat beside Ellman, the Comptroller, a thin man with a cavernous face and skin the color of a fish's underbelly. There were some twenty executives in all. With Harry sitting in for Jim, Bert was the only Black.

"What's it look like?" Bert asked Ellman in a whisper.

"Pretty serious," the other muttered.

The Chairman, a tall, spare man with a ruddy glow and a fringe of grey hair, dressed in a tailored blue serge suit, entered with a grim look. He was in his late sixties, and had retired from the Navy to take over American Instruments.

"All right, men, listen up!" he commanded. "Buckminister, where's my flip chart?"

The plump executive assistant scurried outside and brought back the large pad on a stand, and a pointer.

Admiral Kensington Drake took the pointer, flexed it several times, making a swishing sound, then, pointing it at the Comptroller, demanded, "Why didn't you know about this?"

Bert could feel Ellman's body go rigid beside him.

"They used a law firm as a front," Ellman complained. "They don't have to file with the Securities and Exchange Commission until they acquire five percent of our stock."

"What law firm?" the chairman demanded, scowling.

Dibble, the chief legal counsel, supplied the answer. "Heatherington, Paschall and Fyle. They're based in London. They've a history of fronting for hostile takeovers."

Suddenly, the Admiral's face turned scarlet. "No goddamn limey bastards are going to take over *this company!*" he ended in a scream. "Men, this is war!" he shouted, smacking the flip chart with his pointer. A sharp crack was followed by splinters of wood cascading over the front row of executives.

"Sir," Bert said hesitantly, "maybe we ought to think about selling the European operations. They've lost money for three years now."

"Bullcrap," the chairman retorted. "I'm not letting anyone stampede me into giving away my market. Just what the goddamn Japs want, the slanty-eyed bastards."

Eighteen sets of eyes focused on Joe Fudasaka, the Director of Purchasing, who seemed to be oblivious to the Admiral's tirade.

"Poor bastard," mumbled Ellman, "just got in from Hong Kong this morning, probably still in a fog."

As if to prove the Comptroller's point, Joe's head slid down to his chin.

"Boss," Harry said, "remember, we can't say things like that," indicating the sleeping Joe with his eyes.

"To hell with brotherhood, man, this is war! Dibble, you form a task force to fight this thing. I want your battle plan by three o'clock. Everybody's on twenty-four-hour duty till this emergency is over. Company dismissed." The Admiral stalked out of the office, his assistant at his heels.

"How much do you know about this law firm?" Bert asked Dibble as they walked down the hall.

"I've met one of the partners," the attorney answered, swinging his body aside to let a secretary pass. He was amazingly agile for his three hundred pounds.

"This guy Paschall, what's his first name?"

"Why? Think you know him?" asked the big man, his beady eyes focused on Bert.

"I might."

"I'll look it up," Dibble said, stopping at his office, "and give you a call."

"What happened?" Bridget asked, following him into his office.

"Ah, the old man blew his top—hates the British. Tried to get him to agree to unload the European companies."

She made no move to leave. Then she said, "Harry called. Shall I get him?"

"Yeah, he may know something."

"That was some show this morning," Harry said. "My stockbroker says Stokingham has half of the shareholders in his pocket."

"Nobody really knows. Just a lot of rumors." Bert put his hand over the phone and said, "Nothing new." Bridget shrugged her shoulders and walked out.

"Your buddy, Big Bucks, is grinning all over himself. Claims he predicted this all along—by the way, how was the boat trip?" Harry asked.

"You've got to see that boat to believe it. It was all business—seems the old buzzard's big in real estate."

"Heard he was."

"I mean real big, like having his own banker."

"Wouldn't surprise me. I've seen his apartment building in Queens."

"Here he comes now. Call me if you hear anything."

The gnome swung jauntily through the door. "Looks like retribution day is nigh," he cackled.

"The game isn't over yet, not by a long shot," Bert snapped. "Besides, what'll happen to your shoe shine business?"

The old man dropped to one knee and said, "They'll need shines too. That man's gonna wipe the floor with you all," he continued with a chuckle. "I been tellin' the Chairman for some time now, this company's top heavy—just won't listen."

"Stokingham's no businessman. Name me one company he's run."

The shoe shine man stretched up on his toes. "Seems to know what he's doin', accordin' to what I read. Gets out and finds out what's goin' on, lets the man on the spot run his show. My type of man."

"So do we."

"Sh-e-e-e-t," Bucks said, sitting back on his haunches, "boys in Europe want a pencil, got to ask New York. New man's gonna stop all that shit."

"Whose side are you on anyway? I'm your customer."

"I ain't on nobody's side, just tryin' to warn you. Besides, you ain't bought no product now in some time."

"I still got a whole closet of it," Bert growled.

The shoe shine man added another coat of polish, peered up, and said, "Ever think about real estate?"

"Can't say I have. I understand it's done all right by you. That is *some* boat."

The old man beamed. "Yeah," he said, "Lord's been very good to me. Now I want to get me some class, learn somethin' 'bout art, 'specially ourn. Malik's been teachin' me."

"Dotty tells me you didn't want to pay her."

"Naw, naw," he grinned, sliding up on the credenza. "You don't understand womens."

"She's my wife," Bert said.

"Don't mean nothin'. She from Harlem. Black womens toughest bargainers in the world, when they have a mind to be. Matter of fact, if they ever put their minds to bein' in business we'd have Black business all over."

"Well, that's quite an admission, coming from you. You really believe women are better at business?"

"Hell, any half way smart person knows that. 'Course men ain't gonna admit it, but it's true. Men always lettin' pride get in the way of doin' business. Always got to be boastin' when he got a little somethin'. Never hear womens boast when they got somethin'. Keep it to themselves. That's how they keep what they got.''

"Yeah, well, I'll leave real estate and women to you. I got enough problems with this crazy co-op I live in.''

It was late that evening when Bert joined Henry in his apartment to discuss the co-op's problems. Henry lived on the top floor. He was a bachelor, and literally camped out in his sparsely furnished apartment. "Come in Bert,'' the freckle-faced lawyer said, his button eyes sparkling, a grin from ear to ear.

Bert bit his lip to keep from laughing at the Howdy Doody look-alike.

"We've got to do something,'' Henry exclaimed. "We can't go on like this. Judy's save-the-super campaign was very successful. Almost half the building is with her, including Sol. If you add them to the no-pets-no-pay group, why, that's over half the building not paying rent.''

"Don't the crazy bastards realize the co-op's going to default, and nobody's going to get their investment back?''

"Doesn't seem to register,'' the lawyer responded. "They're convinced that the city or the state will bail us out.''

"That'll be the day.''

"You and I know that, but try convincing them.'' A weary look came over Henry's face.

"Oh hell, why don't we bring Caesar back?'' Bert said in disgust. "They deserve each other.''

"It's not that simple. There'd have to be a full union hearing first. That will last several months.''

"We don't *have* that kind of time. Got any ideas?" He
came closer and murmured, "We'd better talk to the bank
about finding a buyer. I don't know about these nuts, but I
intend to salvage as much of my investment as I can—let
me call the bank. They're in this thing as deep as we are."

Getting up and moving to the window, Bert asked
aloud, "I wonder how in the hell I ever ended up with such
kooks."

"You did the same thing I did, old friend," Henry replied, clasping him around the shoulder. "You were looking for cheap rent. Ain't no such thing." He walked Bert to
the door.

For two weeks the big conference room on the thir-
teenth floor was officially labeled the war room. Commanded
by the overweight attorney, two walls were covered by
multi-colored charts depicting trends in sales, profits, and
capital expenditures. Another wall contained a huge map
of the world, red pins indicating sales offices, blue pins,
manufacturing facilities. A teletype machine in the corner
would come to life spasmodically and spit out a paragraph
or two of financial news. A computer screen flashed the
latest stock prices.

Bert, Dibble, and Ellman sat around the huge conference table in the middle of the floor, surrounded by empty
coffee cups. The door swung open suddenly and the plump
West Indian woman with the thick glasses from the cafeteria wheeled in a cart with doughnuts, coffee, and tea.
Dibble pulled his bulk out of the chair especially built for
him, walked to the coffee wagon, and picked up three jelly
doughnuts with one hand, and a cup of coffee with the
other. He dispatched two of the doughnuts before reaching
his seat. Dibble looked at the other two and announced,

"The old man's getting so feisty I'm afraid to give him our reports. Thought he was gonna punch me yesterday."

"Not our fault," groused Ellman, "the stockholders are going with Stokingham."

"How many?" Bert asked.

"Enough to give him four seats on the Board."

"My God!" Bert exclaimed. "And he still won't sell the European operations."

Ellman nodded his head. He wore a grim look.

"Well, there we sat, fat, dumb, and happy," Dibble said in disgust as he finished his last doughnut and licked his fingers. "No wonder Stokingham sent Paschall after us. Understand he's a real work of art."

Bert suddenly became alert and asked, "Did you ever find out his first name?"

"Yeah—Anton," the chief counsel replied. "Sneaky bastard, so I'm told. Will do anything to find out company secrets."

Bert felt his face burn, said nothing. He wondered how much Anton had gotten out of Bridget, and what would happen if this ever leaked out.

"You look like you've seen a ghost," Dibble said. "You know the guy?"

"No. No," Bert replied, "I was just wondering what we're going to do if Stokingham wins."

"Find a new job," Dibble declared, shuffling the reports in front of him.

"Well, he hasn't won yet," said Ellman. "Let's get on with the job."

Bert raced back to his office as soon as the meeting was over and called Bridget in.

"We've got a real problem."

Her eyes opened wide. "What happened?" she asked.

"Does the law firm of Hetherington and Paschall of London mean any thing to you?"

"Of course," she smiled sweetly. "That's my sweetie's law firm. Why?"

"That bugger's been buying up our stock for Stokingham!" Bert shouted.

"No!" she exclaimed. Her bosom trembled under her no-nonsense blouse. "There must be some mistake." Her face turned scarlet.

"There may be more than one Anton Paschall, but there couldn't be two firms with the same name in London," the executive grimly replied.

A defiant look appeared on her face. "My Anton wouldn't do anything like that."

"What did you tell him about the business?" Bert demanded.

"You actually believe this, don't you?" There was a mixture of anger and hurt in her voice.

"Look, it's a known fact the man goes to any length to find weak spots in the companies his clients want to acquire—he was trying to pump you for information on us, can't you see that?"

"You think that's all he saw in me!" she demanded, standing up.

"There's nothing personal in this!" Bert shouted. "We could both be in a lot of trouble."

"You may be. I'm not," she said haughtily. "I'm not listening to any more of this. I'm going home till you come to your senses."

She almost knocked the shoe shine man over as she strode out the door.

"What you do to her?" Big Bucks asked, sliding his box to the floor.

"Damn woman is crazy," Bert replied.

"Whole place goin' crazy," the old man commented. "Harry's lookin' for another job. Jim leavin' next week."

"That's what Stokingham wants to happen. Divide and conquer. Dirty bastard used his lawyer to get information from Bridget."

The old man looked puzzled.

"The guy she went to London to see is the same guy who bought up the stock for Stokingham."

The old man gave out a long whistle. "Boys play rough, huh?—got to remember that myself," he said, and broke out into a grin.

"Now you see the problem?"

"She ain't told him nothin'," the gnome replied. "She too smart for that."

"You seem to know an awful lot about her," the younger man said suspiciously.

"We jes talks a lot about real estate. Besides, you better be worryin' 'bout your job."

"I'm the only senior Black executive they got. I'm not worried."

"You may be in for a surprise," the old man mumbled, bending over the shoes.

"What do you mean?"

"Nothin', jes lots of us around now."

"You're looking pretty spiffy," Bert said, noticing his pin-striped pants and his white shirt and red silk tie under the brown smock.

"Been to see my man Winston, at Manny Hanny, this mornin'." Daddy paused to put the polish in his box. "Gettin' me a line of credit." A smile lit up his face.

"Planning to join Stokingham in the buy-out?" Bert goaded.

"Naw, that's too rich for me. I stay's with what I know. Plannin' me a pretty big real estate deal. Got my eye on a buildin'. Hector thinks I can get it for a song."

"Hector?"

"Yeah, my accountant."

"Oh, the one who won't speak English? Well, good luck to you."

Bucks paused in the doorway. "Think you ought to apologize to that girl. She didn't mean you no harm."

"Well, I guess it wasn't her fault," the tall executive admitted. "I'll talk to her tomorrow."

CHAPTER TEN

At the breakfast table, Dotty, still in her blue bath-robe, buried her head in the business section of the *New York Times*. The bold headline stared out at Bert, "Chief Executive in suicide leap."

"My God," she said. "To think that anybody would commit suicide over a job."

"It wasn't just a job to him. He was the Chairman. It was his life," Bert replied sadly, taking a waffle off the griddle, the scent of fresh baking rising over the table. Finding it too hot, he dropped it on the table. Dotty speared it with her fork and flipped it onto his plate.

"I guess he's one of them cats that go down with his ship," she observed, pouring another cup of coffee.

"Well, he'd been an admiral—he just couldn't get over the fact that it was a foreign company that took us over. It really got to him."

"He sure made his point," Dotty commented, turning the page. "Diving out of his office window. Damn, I wonder how his wife feels."

"It's a real tragedy." Bert pushed aside his waffle. "Place'll be a zoo."

"What are *you* gonna do?"

"Go to work for the new team, I guess. I'm sure they'll need a planner. Who knows, I may even get a promotion. It's happened—I'll clear and you wash."

"If I were you," Dotty advised, "I'd lay low, and find out what these new cats are all about."

"If you understood corporate life, you'd know that you got to jump in with both boots," Bert responded in a prissy voice.

"By the way, what are you gonna do about Bridget?" Dotty slid the dishes into the soapy water.

"Really doesn't make any difference. We're a division of Stokingham now. Maybe she can put in a good word for me."

"Well, I'll be damned." Dotty put her soapy hands on her hips. "You were ready to fire her last week. Now that the tide's turned, you want her to help *you*."

"That's life," Bert said, turning back to the paper.

"Corporate life, you mean," Dotty snorted, and began to dry the dishes.

Bert was in his office early the next morning. Nine o'clock came and went, and no Bridget. Answering his own phone, he found Harry on the line.

"I can't believe what's going on," Harry said. "What's new?"

"Thought *you* knew," Bert responded.

"I'm too busy job hunting," Harry said. "I hear these Stokingham guys are some pretty hard-nosed bastards. Understand Ellman got it this morning."

"Probably want their own Comptroller," Bert pointed out, a lot more casually than he felt.

"Hold on a second. Big Bucks just came in...says Dibble was fired a few minutes ago."

"Good God!" Bert exclaimed, and his heart began to pound. "Bastards aren't playing—how'd he find out?"

"Gave the new guy a free shoe shine."

"Free! Big Bucks?"

"Better get it from him. I got a job interview in a few minutes."

The phone rang as he hung up. It was Leo. "Mr. Davis, I'm calling for Bridget. She's sick and won't be in for awhile."

"Nothing serious, I hope?"

"Bad case of the flu, doctor said."

"Tell her I hope she feels better." He hung up and was just about to visit Dibble when the shoe shine man walked in.

"She ain't comin' back," the gnome said, motioning his head to Bridget's desk.

"She'll be back," Bert responded confidently.

Bucks didn't answer; he walked over to the painting of the Benin king. "I'll take this off you," he said. "You won't be needin' it."

"What are you talking about?" Bert asked in a startled voice.

"Down talkin' with the new man, Tobias, this mornin'. Already cleanin' out the admiral's junk—man ain't been in his grave a week."

"Why did you assume I'd be fired?"

"Ellman and Dibble gone. Figure you're next. Heard him say he was gonna make a clean sweep. Say y'all responsible for the shape the company's in."

"Hah!" snorted Bert. "I pleaded with the Chairman to get rid of those losers over in Europe."

"Well, I guess he got to keep some of y'all," Bucks said as he bent over Bert's shoes.

"What's he like—" the phone rang and Bert answered it.

"Mr. Tobias would like to see you now," Helen, the admiral's former secretary, told him.

Bert pulled his half-shined shoe off the box, grabbed a legal pad, and left the old man squatting there.

"Good luck," Bucks ventured.

The large oak paneled office had been cleaned out except for the plush chairs and sofa. Clean paint showed where the Japanese flag had hung, and the ship models lay helterskelter in a big cardboard box. Buckminister, the plump administrative assistant who had served the Admiral faithfully, was now busily pouring coffee for Mr. Tobias.

The new President, about forty-five, was very impressive, in a suit tailored to show off his trim figure to full advantage. His small mouth accentuated his beak-like nose. In his breast pocket he wore a handkerchief that matched his powder blue tie, and he waved a cigarette holder when he spoke, with an old world air.

Tobias referred to the file in front of him. "Hmm, good background. I think we can use you." He looked across at Bert from behind his fashionable aviator glasses, took a long pull on his cigarette holder, and blew a long narrow stream of smoke, as if he were making a point.

Bert grinned.

"Of course, you'll report to Brian Murphy. He heads up our planning group—up in Boston."

Bert's grin evaporated.

"Any problems, let Brian know. Look forward to working with you," he said, giving Bert a quick handshake, and turned back to the stack of papers on his desk.

Buckminister herded Bert out of the office and whispered, "Congratulations."

"For what?" Bert snarled, and strode out of the area.

The shoe shine man was reading the *Journal* when Bert returned. He folded the paper and said, "Don't look too happy."

"Bastards!" the younger man shouted, kicking over the waste paper basket. "Just the time you think you're making headway, you get a kick in the ass."

Jackson said nothing.

"You know, it all looks pretty suspicious to me. Just about the time a Black man gets anywhere near the top, they cut him down." The executive sighed. "Now I've got to report to some Irishman in Boston."

"When you gonna learn?" the old man demanded. "All these big corporations alike. All this big talk about equal opportunity—only thing give you equal opportunity is ownin' a business."

"What the hell," Bert said, "I got a meeting with the bank about the co-op in a half hour." He walked out the door with the old man.

"Don't talk to me about real estate," Bert continued as they walked down the hall. "These silly buggers in my co-op won't pay their rent and are about to default. The fact that they'll lose their investment doesn't seem to faze them."

"What y'all gonna do?" the old man asked as they entered the elevator.

"Probably sell out. Better than defaulting and losing our investment."

"Good luck to ya," the old man called as Bert stepped out the front door.

Henry was already in the bank waiting area when Bert arrived. A large blue-and-yellow mural took up one entire wall; a row of secretaries took up the other. As they sat on the blue chrome edged sofa, Bert noticed that several of the secretaries were stealing glimpses of Henry, followed by sly smiles.

"How'd you make out in the takeover?" the redhead asked.

"Still got a job," Bert declared. "I report to some guy in Boston now."

"That's pretty standard in takeovers, isn't it?"

"Mr. Fowler will see you now," the receptionist interrupted, taking one last glance at Henry. "First door on your right."

"Bill Fowler, Bert Davis, our Treasurer," Henry said by way of introduction to the short dark-haired banker, whose narrow shoulders and wide hips resembled a penguin in his dark suit.

"Well, now," said the young man with an owlish look on his face, "you fellows do have a problem, don't you?"

"We," Henry corrected, flashing his winning Howdy Doody. "Bank's in as deep as we are."

Fowler cleared his throat and staring at the file said, "Quite right. The only solution would be an outright sale. As I told you over the phone, one realty firm seems to have gotten wind of your problems. They claim they're prepared to make you an offer."

"Who are they?" Henry asked.

"Wiggins and Wiggins. Don't know 'em, but their balance sheet is quite solid."

"Well, that's what we need," responded Henry.

"It's not gonna be a picnic, if they know we got to sell," Bert pointed out.

Bill Fowler nodded his head vigorously. "However," he interjected, "the bank wants to settle as soon as possible. We've gone along with you people long enough. We won't reject any reasonable offer."

"Yeah, well, we want to salvage our investment," Bert declared.

Henry nodded his head.

"I'll set up a meeting," Fowler responded, getting up and buttoning his suit coat around his huge hips. "I'll be in touch."

Bert found Harry in the cafeteria wearing a dark brown suit with a white shirt and a matching tie. He was stuffing letters into envelopes and gulping down his lunch at the same time.

"My God, aren't we looking conservative. I was planning to take you out on your last day," Bert said, putting down his tray with its ham on rye and coffee.

"No time for California clothes, I'm just glad to be getting out of here," Harry retorted between spoonfuls of soup. "God, the place looks like a morgue."

"It'll settle down," Bert said, looking around the unusually quiet room. "I may be leaving myself, if my new boss and I don't get along. Besides, Bridget quit."

"No kidding. When?" Harry stopped folding and stared at him.

"I got a letter this morning. All it said was, *I quit.* It came by special messenger."

"Well, she was always one for few words. Was it over that lawyer business?" he asked, licking an envelope.

"Yeah, I was pretty ticked off—but it's not like her to just quit like that."

"Well, my friend," Harry said, draining his coffee cup and bunching up his napkin, "I'm on my way. I'm only down the street—let's have lunch sometime. I'm seeing Jim in Chicago next week."

"Give him my best, and good luck," Bert said, trailing him out into the hall.

Bert's temporary secretary was standing in the doorway when he returned.

"A Mister Brian Murphy called while you were out. He's on the phone now."

"Bert Davis," the tall executive announced, sounding as businesslike as possible.

"Hi, Bert, this is Brian. I had to make a quick trip down, and thought we might get acquainted. I'm across the street here at the Pub. Tell you what—why don't you join me in an early lunch here? Know the place?"

"Yes. Be right over," Bert responded. Probably drinks his lunch, he thought.

The Pub boasted dark beams on the ceiling, and an assortment of beer mugs hung over the bar. It was almost empty, except for a fashionably dressed young Black man who was thumbing through a magazine and a young couple who seemed to be on their honeymoon, huddled in a booth kissing.

Bert ordered a drink and watched the door. An older man with a pot belly entered but soon left. After fifteen minutes he looked around the room and checked his watch. Finally, exasperated, he walked over to where the bartender stood and asked, "A guy named Murphy didn't leave a message, did he?"

"I'm Murphy," said a voice behind him.

Bert turned. There stood the Black man with *Time* magazine in his left hand.

"Brian Murphy?"

They both broke into laughter, "Come on," said Brian. "Let's get some lunch."

"My God," Bert said after they were seated. "I thought you were some old fart from Boston."

"Well, they never told *me* you were a brother," the young man said with a smile as he slid into the booth opposite Bert. His speech was very precise, almost effeminate, and he wore a moustache that contrasted with his smooth brown face, a mobile face that telegraphed his moods.

"Why don't we order first?" Brian suggested with a bright smile. The waiter who had followed them back to the booth passed out menus.

"How's the fish?" the Bostonian inquired.

The waiter looked blank.

"Is it fresh?" Brian demanded, his eyes clouding over.

"Everything's fresh," the waiter sniffed.

"One thing you'll learn about me is that I insist on going first class—now, I expect you to continue the way you have," Brian said, after they had ordered. "Your program looks pretty good to me. In fact, there are a couple of things you're doing I'd like to use in our other divisions."

"Thanks," Bert said. "But tell me—how long have you worked for Stokingham? I didn't know they had any Black executives."

"I started in the Aerospace group. It was their first acquisition here in the States. Tobias hired me out of business school."

"Oh ho. He took you right along."

"Yeah, you might say he's my rabbi," Brian finished with a smile.

"Not bad," Bert said admiringly.

"Now then," Brian asked in his precise fashion. "When will you be able to come up?"

"I'd thought of coming up for a couple of days next month, if that's convenient."

Brian's face showed deep puzzlement. "Couple days?" he asked, a little smile playing on his lips.

"What did you mean?" Bert asked, getting a queasy feeling in the pit of his stomach.

His new boss's face grew serious. "I mean," he replied sharply, "I want all my people in Boston."

"Boston?" Bert blurted out.

"Where else?" Brian said stiffly, cutting his fish in precise movements.

"Wait a goddamn minute," Bert roared, his food forgotten. "You're expecting me to pull up and go to *Boston* just like that?"

"Let me put it this way," the younger man said, his face taking on a hard look. "Starting next month, your paycheck will be in Boston."

Bert could feel his legs go weak with anger as he watched Brian continue to cut his food to precise measurements before eating it. Finally, his eyes lifted and met Bert's. "Well, what'll it be?"

Bert threw down his napkin. "To hell with you!" he growled, loud enough to be heard several booths away. Several people stopped to watch as he strode out of the restaurant.

"I told you to stay cool until you found out what these people are all about," Dotty said at supper. The smell of broiling steak made no impression on Bert, who sat dejectedly at the table. She came around behind him and began to massage his neck.

"Can you imagine that snot-nosed little bastard talking to me like that?"

"Lord knows I don't want to go to Boston, but if that's where your job is—"

"It's the way he *said* it," Bert declared. "Cutting his meat like some faggot." He sprang from his seat and began to pace.

"Well, maybe he's tryin' to copy Stokingham's style of being hard-nosed. Might be pretty nice when you get to know him." She set down a bowl of steaming rice.

98

"Ah, he's just a little jerk who thinks he's White because he went to Harvard Business School," her husband replied as he finally sat down and unfolded his napkin.

"Tellin' him to go to hell won't help, not if he's as tight with the new President as you say."

"I wonder." The phone rang. "Ah, hell, I'll get it."

"It was Henry," he informed her, sitting back down.

"What now?"

"We got a meeting with a potential buyer." Bert pushed his untouched steak aside.

"Maybe Boston's not a bad idea. We might need a new place. I can't imagine any new management puttin' up with this nonsense."

"That's if I still got a job—I've never seen one of *us* act like that," Bert said, settling in his leather chair.

"Hah!" she croaked, her mouth still full of steak.

"What's that supposed to mean?" the tall executive asked.

Dotty stood in the kitchen doorway, keeping an eye on the kettle. "You may not remember this, but you were a real pisscutter when you started at American Instruments. At the first Christmas party, Jim took me aside and asked me who you thought you were. Understand the Black employees were thinking about paying you a visit, to remind you of your Blackness."

"Come on," scoffed Bert, "Jim and Harry are always puttin' you on."

"Hah!" Dotty responded.

CHAPTER ELEVEN

Bert had written to Brian telling him he was taking a week's vacation. He was reworking his resume when Henry called.

"We pick up Fowler at the bank at ten o'clock. Then we go to Wiggins and Wiggins. They're on West Twenty-fifth near Eighth."

"That's not much of a neighborhood," Bert commented.

"They sound like an old-line firm—probably been there for years. Fowler claims they have money."

"Okay."

Bert and the red-headed attorney were shown into Fowler's office immediately. The penguin-shaped man tapped the report he was reading with manicured fingers.

"Can't tell you much about them," he said. "Seems they've worked a lot in the slums—Harlem, I mean." He turned scarlet.

"Do you think he can meet our price?" Bert asked.

"No problem about that," the banker assured them in a firm voice, having regained his composure.

"Then let's go," Henry said.

It was a warm fall day; people carried their coats in the bright sunshine. When they reached the street, Fowler flung his hand high in the air and a taxi veered towards the curb where the three men stood. Just as the banker reached for the door, two burly Black workmen in dirty coveralls shoved past him and dove into the back seat. Fowler recoiled in horror, turned, and looked in appeal to Bert, who watched in fascination as one of the laborers, with a wide gap in his teeth, grinned broadly from the cab that pulled away.

Finally, the three men piled into a cab and traveled south towards West Twenty-fifth Street. It was an old building; the foyer was dirty and dismal. A mailwoman, visible through the grimy window, was tying bundles of mail.

A faint order of urine and disinfectant hit them as they entered and searched in vain for the building directory. Then Henry asked the mailperson, "Wiggins and Wiggins?'"

"Fifth," she responded without lifting her eyes.

Suite 560 was a different world; the bright recessed lights brought out the softness of the tan wall coverings, and a deep red rug covered the floor. The receptionist came in from another room. Her tight-knit dress hugged her hips and thighs. Even her big round glasses didn't detract from her pretty face.

"May I help you?" she asked in a prim, high-pitched voice. Her eyes swept the three, finally coming to rest on the tallest one. Then, in a low, sultry voice, she said, "Hi, Bert."

Bert's eyes narrowed. "Cindy? You work here?"

"Sure do," she said, still smiling at him.

Fowler cleared his throat. "We're here to see Mr. Wiggins," he said, handing her his card. "Fowler of Chem-Bank."

Her voice reverted to primness. "Please take a seat. I'll tell him you're here." She swished out of the room, followed by every eye.

Henry grinned. "Where did you meet her, you sly old dog?"

"She's Bucks' girl," Bert replied as all three of them sat on a beige leather couch under an enlarged photograph of an apartment building.

"Bucks? Who's he?" the redhead asked. "I won't tell Dotty."

Fowler grunted. "I talked to a Mr. McIntosh. He's their banker. I don't know if we'll meet the owner himself."

"Which bank?" Bert asked.

"Manufacturers."

"Name sounds familiar...naw, it couldn't be him," Bert said, half to himself, remembering the athletic man on the boat.

"Come right this way," Cindy said from the doorway, a bright smile on her face.

It was a large room; a huge walnut desk and conference table took up almost half of it.

Bert saw the little man, blinked his eyes, and looked again. It couldn't be, he thought. Just then, Winston McIntosh came in grinning.

"Gentlemen," he announced, "Mr. Jackson, Chairman of Wiggins and Wiggins."

Big Bucks nodded at Bert from his leather chair behind the mammoth desk. He was dressed in a dark blue pinstriped suit, a white shirt, and a powder-blue silk tie.

"I'm Fowler of ChemBank. Thompson and Davis of Park West Co-Op."

The old man said nothing, reached over, and pressed the intercom. "Cindy, send Hector in."

Finally, Bert managed to spit out, *"You're* Wiggins and Wiggins?"

"That's my middle name, Wiggins. Peoples respects you when you has a fancy name like that." He seemed quite pleased with himself.

"You two know each other?" Fowler asked.

"Here Hector now."

The short bespectacled accountant had on the same grease-stained palm beach Bert had seen him wearing on the boat.

"These the men representin' the apartment," the gnome said.

"How do you do, sir," Fowler declared, grasping Hector's hand firmly.

Hector blinked at him from behind his tortoise-shell frames.

"Hector don't speak too much English," Bucks said.

Fowler dropped Hector's hand.

Hector grinned at Bert.

"Have you got a spare room we can use?" Bert asked Hiawatha.

"Cindy?" Bucks said over the phone. "Put these peoples where they can talk."

"What's going on?" Fowler demanded when they were alone. "I don't have all day."

"Yeah," Henry said, "how do you know all these people?"

"It's a long story," Bert explained. "You see, the old guy's a shoe shine man down at American Instruments, and this guy Hector's one of the sharpest accountants around. Bucks knows—"

"Bucks?" asked Henry, his button eyes growing larger.

"That's his nickname. What I'm trying to tell you is, this Hector's a real shark. He'll take us to the cleaners."

"How, when he doesn't even speak English?" Fowler demanded.

"Look," said Bert in growing exasperation. "I know all this sounds strange, but believe me, it's true."

"Come on," Fowler said, "they're waiting."

"We're meeting in Hector's office," McIntosh informed them, as they emerged from their confab, then guided them to the office next to Hiawatha's.

Fowler, leading the way, stepped over a stack of accounting journals and muttered, "What a mess." McIntosh hurriedly cleared off three chairs.

The walls were bare except for one large TWA calendar, featuring an airliner flying above the clouds.

Hector sat behind the desk chewing the edges of his huge moustache, his eyes blinking rapidly behind the tortoise-shell glasses. McIntosh perched on a corner of the desk.

"Now then," began Fowler, wearing an ingratiating smile, "most of your buildings are in Harlem, we're giving you the opportunity to break into the upper West Side. We're only asking twelve million. A very fair price, I might add."

Hector suddenly broke out in peals of laughter. He hit the desk with both hands, his glasses falling to the floor.

A wide grin appeared on McIntosh's craggy face.

The trio looked on, in puzzled silence.

Hector, finally composed, retrieved his glasses, picked up a thick file from his desk, turned two pages, and held it so McIntosh could read.

"Well, well," said the athletic looking man, "I see that over half of your tenants don't pay rent."

A wicked grin appeared on Hector's face.

"What kind of price did you have in mind?" Henry interjected.

Hector hurriedly scribbled a figure on a scrap of paper, and handed it to McIntosh. He took a quick look, raised his eyebrows momentarily, and passed it on to Fowler. The penguin-shaped man's face turned crimson. He rose from his chair and shouted, "Six million dollars? What kind of fools do you take us for?"

Hector beamed at the trio.

"Now, now," McIntosh admonished, "let's take it easy, negotations have just begun."

It was four hours later when the three left to go up-town. "That goddamn Hector, he's not content to strip the flesh, he wants bones too," grumbled Fowler, who sat in the middle, his big hips crowding the other two, as the cab moved uptown.

"For somebody that doesn't talk English, he's one tough negotatior," Henry mumbled. "If we took his price, the tenants wouldn't get a dime.

"And *we'd* take a *loss*," the banker said.

"Don't say I didn't warn you," Bert reminded them.

"Well, we're just going to have to get a better price, that's all. The bank is *not* going to take a loss," Fowler ended firmly.

"Neither is this tenant," Bert declared, wriggling his hips for more room and looking out the window at the crowds on the streets.

It was the end of the week. Bert's vacation was almost over when Hiawatha Jackson called.

"I want to talk to you private," he announced. "Sending Malik up for you." The phone went dead.

An hour later, Malik's voice came over the intercom. "I'll wait for you down in the car, my brother."

"Malik, haven't seen you since the boat ride," the executive said as he settled back in the big black Mercedes.

"That's true," the young Muslim replied. "How's the sister?"

"Fine, fine."

"Understand you and brother Jackson are doing business," Malik said with a pleased expression.

"I suppose you could call it that."

"Well, I sure like to see two strong Black men working together."

Bert looked over to see if he was kidding, and remained silent for the rest of the trip.

Big Bucks was alone in his office when Bert arrived. His feet were up on the desk; he pointed to a chair.

"'Cause you my friend," Jackson began, "I gonna offer you a deal."

Here we go, Bert thought.

"Now," said the old man, "I'm prepared to offer you what y'all askin' for that buildin'. Lord knows them tenants got to go."

"What do I have to do?" Bert asked warily, making sure Hector was nowhere around.

"Bucks, could you come out and check this?" asked a familiar voice from outside the door. A smile flickered on the old man's face.

Bucks let out a little giggle. "Come in." Turning to Bert, he added, "Old friend of yourn."

"Bridget?" Bert exploded.

"Hi, Bert," she said, avoiding his eyes. "Just this last part here," she went on, addressing the old man.

"So you're Bucks' secretary now?"

"My manager," Bucks murmured, still reading. Bridget, feeling Bert's stare, adjusted her low cut blouse.

"What I'm talkin' 'bout is you workin' for me," Jackson said after Bridget left. "Jes think, the two of y'all can be together again. Always did make a fine team."

106

Bert recovered from his shock and gasped, "Work for you?"

"Beats goin' to Boston. Harlem girls don't take too well to Boston."

"How'd you find out?" Bert demanded.

"Still shine the boss's shoes."

"Do you know how much I make?" Bert demanded.

"Got a pretty good idea—how much you want?"

"Why me? I know nothing about real estate."

"Got class. Always wanted to have an MBA workin' for me. 'Sides, I need someone like you to represent me."

"What's wrong with McIntosh? Why don't you hire him?"

"Needs a Black man for this," Daddy said with a very serious expression. "Plan to buy up some of this depressed property, mostly Black part of town. Cain't have no White man goin' in there."

Bert stared in amazement at the old man who was busy signing some papers.

"Wouldn't be so surprised if I was White, would ya?" Hiawatha asked looking up.

"No—well, it's just that—"

Bucks rose from his seat and stretched. "You the one sayin' we got the responsibility to hire ourn," a grin came over his wrinkled face. "Now I'm offerin' you a job with a Black company. What you say?"

"I got a job," Bert responded contemptuously.

"Make you Vice-President."

The younger man remained silent.

"First thing, I wants a art gallery. Malik knows all about that. Don't answer now," the old man said firmly. "'Scuss it with the wife."

Malik appeared out of nowhere and guided a stunned Bert to the car.

BOB WAITE

It was late in the evening when Bert entered the small restaurant around the corner from the hospital. Anne, the wife of the owner, waved him to an empty table.

"She should be in any time. Want a hot cider while you wait?"

"Thanks, Anne, it's getting cold out there."

Bert could see into the kitchen from where he sat. He watched Cliff, the owner, a short, rotund West Indian who was busily preparing the dishes for the evening. The smell of spice and frying foods whetted his appetite.

"This ought to hold you—here she comes now."

"Hi, Anne. Taking care of my sweety?" Dotty asked, taking off her coat. "Gettin' cold out there." She reached over and kissed her husband on his bald spot.

"Got beef patties tonight?" Bert asked Anne.

She nodded. "Just out of the oven."

"How does it feel to loaf all day?" Dotty asked, helping herself to her husband's hot cider.

"I was down at Bucks' place again."

"Again? What for?"

"Would you believe? That bugger had the gall to offer me a *job!*" Bert exploded loud enough to attract the attention of the next table.

"A job?" echoed his wife. "Doing what? Shining shoes?"

A pained expression came over Bert's face.

"I'm sorry, honey," she said, taking his hand in hers, "I just couldn't resist it."

"He had the nerve to offer the co-op a better deal if I went to work for him. Can you believe that? *Me* work for *him.*"

"What's he payin'?"

"That's not the point!" Bert exclaimed.

"Isn't that what you captains of industry supposed to do? Buy and sell each other?"

108

"You're not funny," Bert responded, and proceeded to relate the events of the day.

"Sounds like a pretty good offer to me, all things considered. I know he's a rascal, but no different than that crew down at American Instruments."

"I can't work for him," Bert said indignantly.

Anne deposited the plate of appetizers. "Take your time. I'll come back for your order."

"These smell great," Dotty exclaimed. Then a sly smile crept over her face. "I know what's bothering you, Mr. Macho. You don't want to work on the same level with your old secretary. Shame on you."

Bert gritted his teeth and said nothing.

"Come on, 'fess up, that's what it is—mmm, these taste great." The scent of the pastry-wrapped meat pies covered the table.

"Both you and Bucks seem to forget I still have a job and a very good one at that," he snapped.

"After you told your boss to go to hell?"

"Oh, I'm sure we'll come to some accommodation."

"Have you decided?" the waitress asked, pencil poised.

"I'll take the honeyed chicken," Dotty answered.

"Make mine the same...I don't know if I have much of a choice," Bert sighed. "I can either opt for Boston— that's if I still have a job—and lose our investment in the co-op. Or I work for Bucks."

"I understand the problem," Dotty said, biting into a patty. "What you gonna do?"

"You want to go to Boston?"

"That's not the issue. I'll go wherever you go. The question is, do you want to work for Bucks? You're the one always saying we ought to stick together. Maybe it's time you worked for a Black company."

Bert snorted.

109

The couple had just reached their front door; Dotty saw it first—a yellow corner sticking out under the door.

"Oh my God it's a telegram, I just know somebody died."

Bert tore it open. It read, *Don't bother to come to Boston. Report to Personnel.* It was signed by Brian.

"Who?" Dotty demanded, her face ashen.

"I've been fired."

The wind slammed the door shut after the couple entered.

When Dotty turned to face him, tears were streaming down her face. "Those bastards," she said fiercely. "I'm ready to take 'em all on—after all you've given them."

Bert gathered her in his arms and said, "We knew it was coming."

"You're taking it very casually," she sniffed.

"Maybe Big Bucks is right after all."

"Meaning what?" Dotty asked, looking up at him.

"Maybe I *should* be in real estate."

For additional copies
write to:

Daddy Big Bucks
802 Columbus Drive
Teaneck, NJ 07666

— — — — — — — — — — — —

Please send me _____ copy(ies) of **Daddy Big Bucks**
@ $7.95 each, including postage and handling.

All orders must be prepaid by check.

Name _____

Address _____

City _____ State _____ Zip _____